Sometimes Art Can't Save You

Jill L. Ferguson

IN YOUR FACE INK LLC

Glendale, AZ · 2005

This book is a work of fiction. References to real people, events, establishments, organizations, or locales are intended only to provide a sense of authenticity, and are used fictitiously. All other characters, and all incidents and dialogue, are drawn from the author's imagination and are not to be construed as real.

In Your Face Ink LLC
9524 W. Camelback Road
#130-182
Glendale, AZ 85305
Tel: (623) 570-1072
www.inyourfaceink.com

Printed in the United States of America
First Printing: October 2005
ISBN 0-9765659-1-9
Library of Congress Control Number on file.
Ferguson, Jill L.
Sometimes Art Can't Save You

Design and Typesetting: Edward J. Kamholz

To everyone who has been used, abused or has felt
invisible

Acknowledgements

This book would not be possible without the unwavering support of my husband Darren, who believed in the project from the beginning and allowed Jessica to consume our lives for a period of time. Special thanks to the Writing Goddesses—Debbie, Heather, Laura, Margie and Vandy— who read, re-read and edited endless drafts, and to my many students who listened and offered feedback on the first few chapters. Your help was appreciated.

Groups like Self-Injurers Anonymous (www.selfinjurers.com) and Showing Our Scars (www.showingourscars.org) are incredible resources for individuals and friends and family members dealing with self-injury. I am grateful for their thorough information and for the help and hope they provide.

RAINN (Rape, Abuse & Incest National Network, www.rainn.org and 1-800-656-HOPE) offers counseling, support, prevention tips and resources 24 hours a day, seven days a week for those who have been sexually assaulted. They are an invaluable organization.

All characters and situations, though they represent reality, are fictitious. Any errors of fact are my own.

Someone once said to create great art, the artist must suffer. Well, I had seen enough suffering in my sixteen long years to last a lifetime. I created artwork so much my mom's buzz-cut blonde boyfriend constantly complained to her: "Jessica's in there with her damn paints again." He didn't understand. To be an artist one must commit oneself to art. One must see art, breathe art, be art. My bedroom was crowded with easels. Paints, canvas, pastels, paper, pen, ink, almost any medium covered my bed, small desk, and all of the floor. I probably could have opened a drive-thru art supply store from my bedroom window. Art and art supplies were the first things I saw when I awoke in the morning, and the day's latest project was the last thing I saw before I went to bed. I only left my studio for food, water, and the necessary trips to the bathroom.

It was summer so I didn't have to leave to go to school. Instead, when I felt the need for inspiration—usually once a day—I would head to the art museum. I had bought a yearlong pass with my babysitting money. The docents and security people all knew me by name, so I could lose myself there for hours with my sketchpad, concentrating on my art, blocking out the rest of my miserable existence.

Occasionally, Ethel, my favorite purple-haired docent, would come by and bring me cookies and an iced tea. Food and beverages were forbidden outside the museum's café, but exceptions were often made for me, although I never asked to be singled out and excused from the rules. I guess they just all thought I was too skinny. Ethel would sit with me and talk about the great works of the masters in her lilting, soft voice that always reminded me of the brook we'd lived near in Wisconsin. She wasn't from around here either, but had been dragged to L.A. when her husband died so she could be closer to her son. He was some big movie producer who didn't really have time for her, but eased his conscience by buying her a big condo and getting her this job. She was a retired art teacher so I guess it was fitting, but sometimes I wondered if she wouldn't have been been happier back in Louisiana painting and playing bridge with her friends.

Ethel loved to watch me work. She told me once that I was one of the best artists my age she had ever seen. I thanked her and felt good for a few seconds, replaying her words in my head. The only problem was I didn't want to be one of the best artists my age. I wanted to be one of the best artists PERIOD. I wanted shows in New York and L.A. and San Francisco and London. I wanted art reviewers to write me up in the finest of magazines and newspapers saying things like my "paintings possessed a raw, vibrant energy so lacking in today's art". I wanted to be the latest and greatest thing. The "It girl" of the art world. I wanted more than my fifteen minutes of fame. Did I have to cut off my ear to get it?

Instead I pressed on, painting and pining after my muse. I slept little and ate little all summer. The demons of doubt came at night, when I closed my eyes, so I fought sleep. Just one more brushstroke, I said to myself, and it will be brilliant and I would be brilliant, not just some stringy haired, underdeveloped, too-tall teen. But one brushstroke led to another and then another, and pretty soon the canvas was hosed. Not even a hint of my original dream, my original art. I'd rip the canvas from its frame, shredding it, while tears of blind rage ran rivers from my eyes.

Eventually, exhausted, I cried myself to sleep only to be awakened a few hours later by nightmares too horrible to remember.

In the morning, after wiping my crusty, swollen eyes, I painted hairy, muscular, masculine hands reaching into a black hole towards a beating, bleeding heart. A masterpiece. Almost as good as the disturbing one I did two years ago full of angry reds and muted, mutilated flesh.

Then, I knocked on my mother's bedroom door and entered at her beckoning. I wanted to share my painting with her. She and Jim were still in bed, covers pulled up to their chests. Jim was still asleep. That's when I noticed them. Jim's hands. They were like the ones in my painting, the ones from the nightmare I refused to remember. They were large and muscular, with lots of blonde hair on them. I almost turned and ran from the room, but my mother asked to see the painting. She took one look at the painting and proclaimed it my best work yet. I could have told anyone she would say that. She always said it. I am not even sure she really looks at any of them. I mumbled thanks and fled the room.

I stashed the canvas in my room and then ran the shower extra hot. I wanted to wash the paint, the grime, the feelings, and memories down the drain. I closed my eyes under the water and the tears came again. My mother was so happy, so in love now, and she deserved it. It was not easy to rebuild your life when someone you loved blew his brains out. In many ways I was glad she had Jim. I was glad he took her away from Wisconsin, away from the nightmares. I just wished I could get away from him, from them. She didn't need me anymore, really. I was just a trigger to past memories best left forgotten.

I stepped out of the shower, wrapped a towel around my head, and put my old dingy gray terrycloth robe around my body. I peered into the mirror. My eyes looked sunken, with charcoal rings around them. Damn, I forgot to remove my mascara again. I picked up my mother's makeup that sat on the back of the toilet. She had more eye shadow colors than Rite-Aid. I added blue and pink and brown to the charcoal rings. I created shadows and light on my flesh canvas. I drew zigzags with lipstick and circles with eyeliner. I applied dots in shiny black mascara. I needed red. Not carmine or light red, but a really red red. I picked up the straight-edged razor from the back of the sink—one of Jim's left over appliances from his military days in Special Forces. I sliced my wrist slightly, to the right of the scar, not enough to kill myself, just enough to draw blood and make it hurt. God that felt good. I smeared some of the blood onto the made-up mess that was my face.

Perfect. A masterpiece.

I scurried from the bathroom to my bedroom, not wanting my mother and Jim to see me, knowing they wouldn't understand. I picked up the instant camera inside my nightstand and aimed it at my face. I pushed the button and waited for the picture to appear. I needed more light for the picture to turn out right. I positioned myself under a halogen lamp and snapped another instant. This one had the proper lighting. I picked up my good camera and shot half a roll, making different faces for each frame.

After cleaning my face, dressing, and grabbing a granola bar, I yelled that I was headed to the museum. No one objected; they never do. Today was Saturday. They would spend half the day in bed, probably glad I was gone. I stopped at the drugstore and dropped off the film. If the photos turned out how I hoped, they would be perfect for the mixed media series I wanted to do.

Hours later on the way back from the museum I stopped at the drugstore to pick up the pictures. I handed my numbered receipt to the female behind the counter. She barely glanced at it as she turned to the clear rubber container stacked with envelopes of developed film. I thought she was about 20, and she was Asian with long, shiny black hair, almost to her waist. I saw her eyes get wide when she matched my number to my name. She turned back to me with a shocked look on her face; her pale skin blanched even paler. I already had out my money, afraid that this would happen. She kept her eyes averted even when she placed my change in my palm. "Thanks. Nice hair," I mumbled as I quickly scooted to the door. She obviously didn't know real art when she saw it.

It was killing me, but I waited to look at the photos until I was safely locked in my room. I didn't want some weirdo on the bus peering over my shoulder, spying on my work and my life. I raced into the house and ran past the closed door of my mom's room. Big surprise—they were still in there. At her age…that's gross.

When she and Jim finally emerged, he usually went out in the evening to get the paper, while my mom acted all giddy like some of my stupid classmates, the ones who act all girly and whispery. The ones I wished would grow up. Well, my mom, she would confide in me—about shit I didn't want to know. Shit I shouldn't know.

Anyway, I don't want to think about that. As soon as I turned the lock, I tore open the envelope and spread the pictures out on my bed. Damn, some of them were good— downright eerie. I looked possessed in one and completely evil in another. In another I looked more depressed than a sad clown. What a range of emotions! If they gave an Emmy for photographic acting, I should get it. I arranged the pictures into a line, one stacked under another, all the way down the bed. I rearranged them and stacked them again, trying to get a sequence going.

Then I formed them into a giant circle—a circle of twenty-five rectangles—in the center of my bed. Yes, that was the way it should look, the way they ought to be displayed when I get a show. Emotions are circular not linear. They go around and around and around and around, repeating endlessly, sometimes displaying vivid colors like my morning masterpiece, and sometimes more subdued like the facial painting of pastels I did the day before.

I pulled out small white stickers from my desk, grabbed a pen and started to number the photos. I gave each photo a sticker with a number, arranged them in a pile, and then put them back in the envelope. Finally, I placed the envelope into my bottom desk drawer, the locked drawer at the bottom with all of my other photos.

I heard the door of my mom's room open and then the front door slam. I looked out the window to see Jim getting into his Porsche. My mother's soft knock sounded on my door.

"Honey?" she called.

"What?"

"Will you open the door?"

I did as she asked and met her eyes. She stood dressed in tight jeans and an even tighter sweater. At least she wasn't wearing high heels; then she could have walked the boulevard.

"How was your day?" She crossed into my room and sat on the bed.

"Fine. The museum was pretty empty." Idle talk with an idle mind, as far as I was concerned.

"Oh, that's good. Jim's gone for the evening. I thought maybe we could hang out together, watch a movie, get a pizza, give each other facials or something, you know, have a girls' night, like we used to." She smiled showing two rows of newly bleached teeth.

Ugh! Why should we?

She looked at her perfectly manicured nails and said, "We haven't done anything together for so long, so I thought if you weren't busy…" she let the sentence trail off.

I couldn't believe she sounded like she genuinely wanted to spend time with me. But wait, maybe it was just a trick so she could talk about Jim. "Umm…" I said, wanting to stall, trying to figure out what to do.

"Well, we don't have to," she said. "It was just a thought." She arose and headed toward the door.

"No, wait. Maybe we could…what did you want to see?" I realized I actually felt nervous about this. It was my own mother, dammit, not a date or something. Why were my palms sweating?

"You can pick the movie, or we don't have to watch a movie. We can go out to dinner or do whatever you want."

I was puzzled. What day was it? My birthday? No, that wasn't it. Months had passed since I had done anything with my mom. At least months. I think it had been since she and Jim hooked up. What the hell was going on?

"Are you okay, Mom?"

"Sure. Why wouldn't I be?" She was still standing in the doorway, looking down at the carpet, while balancing her weight on one foot and then the other.

"I dunno." I mumbled while thinking, maybe because you all of a sudden want to spend time with me after we haven't talked for more than ten minutes a day for the last year or more.

As if she read my mind she said, "I know that we haven't spent much time together, honey, but I want to make up for that. I miss you. Let's take tonight to get reacquainted." Her eyes actually looked misty.

Part of me wanted to believe her, to trust her.

I remembered all of the fun times we had together, when it was just the two of us, laughing, shopping at the mall, playing with make-up; I couldn't refuse.

"Uh, okay. Let's order a pizza and rent a movie." Indoors seemed the safest, because I could always retreat to my room. And besides, I wasn't too sure I wanted to be seen around town with her dressed that way, even though it was no different than usual.

We watched a movie and ate a vegetarian pizza (my choice), and the evening wasn't half bad. It was weird though.

She barely mentioned Jim, and she seemed distracted. I hoped they hadn't had a fight. As much as I didn't want to be here, I didn't want to move back to boring old Wisconsin either. Too many ghosts and ghoulish relatives. Plus, I never missed the winter—all that snow and ice and shit. Though, on the other hand, I could stand a school closing now and then.

Anyway, Jim didn't come home that night, which was strange. He had never been away overnight before, at least not since they had gotten together.

I asked about it, but all my mother did was mumble something about "business."

*What*ever.

If she didn't want to tell me that was okay. I was just happy not to have to listen to the gory details for once. After the movie was over, she asked if I wanted a facial or to go for ice cream or something. A new ice cream place had opened just around the corner. It was one of those places where you picked the flavor from a short list, and some toppings and then they pounded the hell out of the ice cream and toppings, mooshing them together and sometimes even throwing the ice cream spatulas, complete with the mooshed mess, into the air and at each other. It was like some freaking synchronized ice cream circus show.

Anyway, I loved going there and watching them. In a way, they were creating ice cream art. But, to be seen there on a Saturday night, a date night, at around midnight with your mom, is so uncool. I had to pass. I made some lame excuse like I really wasn't in the mood for ice cream and said maybe I'd just go to bed. Mom looked disappointed, but I didn't know what she really wanted, what was really going on. Sometimes, I thought I was better off not knowing, so I quietly shut the door to my room, turned on the stereo, and started to sketch.

2

The next morning, Jim still wasn't home and when I got up there was a note from Mom saying she'd gone to the gym. That was another of her new obsessions. She spent almost as much time molding her muscles as she did in bed with Jim. I guess that wasn't all bad. I mean, if she was going to wear those tight clothes, I would rather her look hot to my friends than all polyester-and-rolls-of-fat disgusting.

She kept asking me to go with her. I told her I didn't need to. I got enough exercise during the school year in gym class. Don't laugh. I know gym's a joke, but she doesn't know that. Besides, I already looked like a stick. What would be the point?

I shouldn't have asked.

She told me the adrenaline high from working out was almost as good as the best mind-blowing orgasm.

Ugh! Could she be more embarrassing!

At least now she has stopped asking and taken to leaving notes, and I don't have to see her parading around in all that bright colored Spandex.

I had to admit though that she was looking good, but don't ever tell anyone I said that. My grandmother once told me that if I developed a chest, I could be as attractive as my mother. I told her when I get older, maybe I'll buy myself one. She didn't appreciate that answer and told me to be patient, that it would happen to me soon enough.

Well, I am still waiting. I even stick my thumbs in my mouth and blow them occasionally. Grandma told me that would help. I know it's crap, but I figure, what the hell, doesn't hurt anything. And, though I hate to admit it, when I was younger, after reading that Judy Blume book about that girl Margaret, I even did those lame we-must-increase-our-bust exercises for a few weeks. All that got me was looking like a funky chicken in the mirror and some sore chest muscles.

I figured while I had the house to myself— and I knew it would be hours before Mom returned, as she worked out longer than anyone else except maybe Arnold Schwarzenegger—that maybe I could call the neighbor to come over for a little while. See, we had this agreement. His name was Timothy, and while we weren't into each other, we were experimental—just like my art. Sometimes he'd pose for me, sometimes I'd have him paint my naked body with acrylics and then I would roll around on a very large canvas. And, if things got a little crazy from there, whatever.

I trusted him. Him, and very few others.

So, I called.

He wasn't doing anything and came over. Made me wonder if he saw my mom leave and was hoping for this. He rarely called first. Sometimes I think he didn't really know what to think of me or of what we did together. But, he was very quiet and didn't have a whole lot of friends, kind of a loner like me, so I knew he was trustworthy.

I asked if I could paint his body and photograph it. He didn't even respond, just started stripping. I had already spread a sheet on my bedroom floor and locked the door, so I just grabbed handfuls of slippery, thick paint—blues and greens and blacks and oranges—and started running my paint-covered hands up and down his body. He was actually holding his breath.

"What's wrong?" I asked, feigning innocence.

"Nothing." It was almost a gasp, not really a word.

I noticed he was getting hard, but purposely ignored that part of his body. I picked up a handful of yellow and smeared it on his left leg, from ankle to knee. I did the same with red paint on his right leg.

"I'm missing something," I said. His eyes got wide. "Be right back."

I unlocked the door, threw it open, and ran to the kitchen. I returned with oatmeal, golden honey, and Chex.

"What the hell?" he asked, eyebrows arched, eyes popping.

"It's okay," I said and grabbed his hand. "Just sit down. No, lay down on your back. It will wash off when I'm done."

"I don't know, Jess…"

"It's okay," I said, and pecked his cheek. "It won't hurt, I promise."

"But—"

I placed my index finger across his lips. "Shh, just be quiet and lie still."

He did as he was told.

I started with the honey first and drizzled some over his

stomach and then I sprinkled the oatmeal. It made swirling patterns in the honey, sticking.

I painted his private parts in green and yellow. I picked up the burnt sienna and applied that to his nipples. Then I wiped my hands on my paint-stained apron and grabbed the camera. I took one picture of his whole body while I stood on my bed. That's the only way I could get enough perspective to get him from head to toe. His facial expression remained blank.

Then I got closer and started to rapidly snap pictures of his parts—of my artwork. The oatmeal, honey, paint picture seemed like it would show the cool texture. I hoped it would translate onto the film. He asked if I wanted him to do anything, to move any way.

I said no. After a dozen varied shots, I said, "Stay there." I quickly undressed and spread white and purple paint onto my belly and chest. Then I lay down on top of him and squirmed around mixing my paint with his paint and food mixture. He put his arms around my back.

"Not yet," I said, pushing his arms away. I stood up and grabbed a canvas from the corner. I looked at my chest and stomach: quite a mixture of brilliant colors and lumpy textures. I lay down on the canvas, making an imprint of my body. There were colorful small circles where my boobs were, a barely round smudge where my flat belly touched the canvas, and even some squiggly green lines where my pubic hairs must have picked up the paint from Timothy.

I picked up the honey and squirted a diagonal line of it across the canvas. I grabbed a handful of Chex from the box and threw them at the canvas. The ones that hit the honey embedded and stuck. I grabbed a can of spray adhesive, aimed, and pushed the aerosol button, covering the canvas in clear sealer.

"Okay, now," I said to Timothy, who had shifted onto his side with his head resting on his hand propped up by his elbow. He had been watching me. "Unless you want to shower. We can do it in the shower, if you want."

He smiled and reached towards me. "Or we can do both." He grabbed a condom from his jeans pocket. His smirk said it all.

After Timothy left and I had dried my hair and dressed again, I sat on my bed, mesmerized by the art we had completed. The canvas leaned against my far wall, the one I had painted a dull black from floor to ceiling. The colors and texture leapt from the canvas against the black background. I'd have to remember to put this painting against black cloth when I had my show.

I wondered when my mother was coming home and if I should be here or not. Jim still hadn't come home and I didn't know what kind of mood that would put her in. My sinuses were stuffy—maybe from all the cheese on the pizza last night—so I popped a Benadryl and swigged it down with some water from the cup on my nightstand.

Benadryl. That brought back memories of another embarrassing discussion I had had with my mother. Actually, it wasn't really a discussion since she did all the talking and I did all the cringing. One time, about a year ago, I was having an allergy attack and she gave me an anti-histamine. I had just popped the pill in my mouth and put the glass of water up to my lips when she said, "Don't ever take one of these before sex. Dries up all your membranes, so the experience won't be pleasurable. Remember that." I choked on the damn pill and mouthful of water. Where did she get this stuff?

But you know what, it was true. I checked it out on the

Internet. I mean, you don't want your mother saying shit like that to you, but it is good information to know. So, I checked it out and she was right. That was why I didn't take the allergy med before I called Timothy. I knew what we'd be doing, and even though I was not into him or anything, I still wanted it to feel good. I mean, if it doesn't, what's the point? Right?

My mom returned around 1:30 with a huge smile plastered on her face. She rushed into the house calling my name. That was a new one. I actually responded. She raced into my room. "You'll never believe who was at the gym, honey. Angelina Jolie. She's even more buff in person. And those tattoos. I never knew they could be so sexy. I'm thinking I should get one. What do you think? On my ankle, my bicep, my hipbone? Where do you think?"

I just stared. I couldn't believe it. Any of it. That she saw Angelina or that she was talking to me about getting a tattoo. Kids in my school got tattoos, not moms.

"Well, what do you think? Where should I get one, and what kind do you think would be sexy? Maybe I should get Jim's name tattooed on my chest, right over my heart." She stood looking in the mirror over my dresser, stretching her Spandex down past her left boob. I think she was trying to visualize it.

I had to interrupt. "Mom. You don't need a tattoo." I took a big gulp of air before the next statement, steeling myself. "You are cool without one." I couldn't believe I actually made that line sound feasible. And I didn't gag or snicker.

"But everyone has tattoos." She turned and looked at me.

"Yes, but you're not everyone. How 'bout if I paint something on you and you can see if you like it first? Before you move on to something more permanent." Now I felt like the freakin' parent.

She actually squealed with delight and plopped down on my bed.

"Calm down, or I won't do it," I said, giving her my stern look. "Where do you want it? I think the hip bone would be good." And the least visible, I thought, as long as she doesn't start flashing people.

"Oh, that's a great idea," she said, and started pulling down her clingy shorts. "So, Jim's name? A butterfly? What do you think?"

"A butterfly might be cool," I responded, thinking she's often as flighty as one. Or maybe she's more like a hummingbird. No, she's too obsessive when she finds something she likes. A bird wouldn't work. "How 'bout a tiger's head? Or a simple flower?"

"A rose. A yellow rose. I've always liked yellow roses." She said this with a finality that made me think she had made up her mind.

"Okay, a yellow rose it is. Do you want to shower first, while I mix up the various yellows that we'll need?"

"No need, sweetie, I showered at the gym. I just changed back into Spandex because it's so comfortable." She smiled.

Oh great! A whole day with my mother in workout clothes. I put little dabs of yellow on my palette and then a dot of other colors—brown, white, umber, etc.—next to every dab but one. This would be the most beautiful rose anyone would ever lay eyes on—if anyone ever really would. Well, at least I would photograph it a few times so I could have a permanent reminder of it—and of this weird day.

"Now, lay back on the bed and let me work," I said. She

did as she was told and actually kept quiet and still the whole time too.

I must admit: it was another masterpiece. The rose was almost perfect, so much so that it looked three dimensional and real. I took many pictures.

She was pleased with the results and gave me a hug, which startled me. I shrugged her off and told her I was glad she liked it, but that I had work to do, plus I had to babysit in a few hours. I needed to get some stuff done. She mumbled that she understood and traipsed back down the hallway to the kitchen.

I wished Jim would return so she would quit spending time with me. I wasn't used to it anymore. It was weirding me out.

I closed my bedroom door, lay back on my bed and listened to music with my eyes closed, mentally creating my next collage.

Jim came home the next afternoon, making Mom and me much happier. Now I didn't feel so much like I had to entertain my mother. I could get back to life as usual. He brought back a t-shirt for me from Maui, which is apparently where he went. He didn't really give it to me. I just came home from the art museum and found it laying on the back of my desk chair. It was black (just like I like my clothes to be) and had Maui in muted yellow letters across the chest. After inspecting it closely, I carried it out to the living room where Jim and Mom were both sitting on the couch engaged in a deep conversation, and said, "Hey, thanks."

Their heads snapped toward me in unison, making it almost comical. Jim started to say, "You're welcome," but I had already turned and started walking down the hall. I didn't mean to interrupt them.

"Wait, Jessica," my mother said. "We need to talk to you."

Oh no. Not the words I wanted to hear. I hesitated, but came closer and faced them. They looked at each other and

I guessed somehow one told the other that Mom should go first, though that part was lost on me.

"Sit down." She motioned to the lounge chair.

I sat.

"So, we've been talking. Jim was in Maui scouting condos and townhouses because he wants to buy a few, maybe as investment property. He found one he wants me to see. Actually, us to see, if you want to go."

I stared, confused. "Huh?"

My mother continued, "Maui is a great place to buy investment property and new places are being built all the time. Jim has money to invest and wants us to see what he's buying before he does. He wants our opinions. Plus, he asked if you would help decorate it. He likes your artistic flair."

Part of me was flattered and I am sure that showed by the smile plastered on my face. I mumbled, "Thanks, Jim," but my eyes didn't really meet his.

"So, what do you think? Do you want to leave next week for Hawaii? We can make it a family vacation."

Just what I wanted: a family vacation. Yippee! I didn't think they could be serious. First they don't really include me in their lives for over a year and now they want to take a family vacation? What the hell would we all do together? And for how long? The last question I repeated aloud.

"Well, how long do you want to go for?" Jim asked. "I mean, if I am buying some places, we can stay as long as we like. A few days, a few weeks, maybe even the rest of the summer if you want." He smiled and must have been thinking this would make me happy.

I was speechless. The idea of getting away sounded good, but would I be able to create viable art in Maui? What about all my paints and things? Could I take them with me? With airline restrictions I wasn't sure I could bring oil-based paints and solvent and spray adhesive with me on the plane.

"You can bring a friend, if you want," my mother added.

Friend, what friend? I didn't have any friends. Had she ever seen one of my friends, beyond Timothy's occasional visits? I thought the paint tattoo I gave her must have seeped bad stuff into her brain.

I was perplexed and didn't know what I wanted. I started to get up from the chair. "Let me think about it," I said over my shoulder as I ran to my room and shut the door. I don't know what they expected from me, but this whole thing was just weird, so weird it made me cry.

The next morning, I emerged from my room with my eyes all puffy from the night before. I had made up my mind, but needed a shower before I faced them. Their door was still closed, which was good. I could head to the shower unimpeded and get myself prepared—physically and mentally—to go make a deal with them. I'd go to Maui with them for a week max. And if I couldn't take my paints with me, Jim would have to buy me new ones when we got there—at least enough of them to get me through those few days, and some canvases too. I could pack my smaller folding easel into my luggage. Also, Mom would have to take me to get a new swimsuit, or on second thought, give me money for one, as I didn't want her tagging along on the shopping spree. She'd just be embarrassing and our tastes were nothing alike. If they'd agree to that, then I'd go. Otherwise, they could leave me here and not worry about me, nothing too different from usual, and fine by me.

The few days before we left for Maui were some of the weirdest I remember. I didn't think my mother and Jim would get through them intact. My mother was taking this trip very seriously, or at least the clothing part of the trip. She shopped and shopped and then shopped some more. Every time she returned with bags from Nordstrom's and Macy's and Saks and Bloomies, she would lug her packages to her room and start a fashion show for me or Jim or whomever else was around.

One day she came home with about six bags stuffed with stuff. She yelled "hello" and then raced into her room. Jim was already in there with the door shut. I heard some muffled talking and that was about all. But I wasn't really paying attention. Timothy was over, legitimately this time— or at least, I mean, Jim and my mom knew about it. He was sitting for me while I painted his portrait in acrylics. Of course, what I was painting didn't exactly look like him. I mean, if you knew Timothy you would know it was a like-ness of him, but instead of his pale flesh-color and freckles, I gave him washed-out red skin and purple freckles and green hair and yellow eyes, my wild interpretation of him.

Anyway, I was busy painting and wasn't paying much attention to what was going on in my mom and Jim's room. All of a sudden, the door burst open and my mom came trotting down the hall in these clear, Plexi-glass-looking high heels and the teeniest, tiniest bathing suit I had ever seen. And she was walking towards us. Timothy's eyes bugged out of his head like he was a cartoon character. Oh great, I thought. Now my mother just became part of his spank bank. Just what I needed. The only guy I was screw-ing and now when he was whacking off he'd be thinking about my mom. Ick!

"What do you think?" Mom asked, spinning around so we'd get the picture. Not that I needed or wanted to see that much of her. The bathing suit, and I use that term loosely as I can't see her really bathing in that piece of dental floss, was leopard print. It was a g-string, with a string bra and two tiny triangles of fabric that barely covered her nipples.

"Oh, Mom!" I sighed.

Timothy must have found his voice because he quietly said, "Looking good, Mrs. Vandermeyer." I almost expected him to whistle but he didn't. He didn't have the nerve.

My mother placed her hands on her hips. Her face wore a huge smile. "Now, Tim, I have told you many times before. I am not Mrs. anyone, especially now. Karen is just fine."

I could tell Timothy was trying to keep his eyes on my mother's face and not look anywhere else. I knew it was a struggle for him and I wanted to laugh. "You look nice," he said and his voice cracked a little.

Just then Jim came out of the bedroom. "Christ, Karen. I didn't know the boy was here. Put some clothes on. You can't parade around like that."

She turned so we were now looking at her butt. "Why not? I will be parading around the beach like this. Besides, I'm in my own home and in my own home I'll do what-ever the hell I want."

"Not while the neighbor kid is here you won't." Jim's fiery eyes stared her down.

Timothy and I just gaped at the two of them. I was used to it; he wasn't, so his eyes were big and he looked a little frightened. Timothy's mom was single and had always been. It was just the two of them so he never got to see adults fight.

"I look great and I'll wear whatever I damn well please!" My mother started down the hall and tried to push past Jim. He grabbed hold of her arm and steered her into the bedroom. The door slammed.

Timothy turned and looked at me and whispered, "Is she going to be okay?"

"Sure. They fight all the time. The thing is, Jim wants her to look sexy to make other guys jealous, but he doesn't want her to look too sexy, or maybe sleazy is a better word for it. He wants guys to envy what they think he has. When she puts it all out there like that, there's no guess work."

"Yeah, definitely no guesswork when you can pretty much see all the parts." He smirked, remembering.

I slapped his arm. "Stop that! That's my mom you're thinking about. I know she encourages it, and even welcomes it with her clothes…or lack thereof…but don't think about her that way. It creeps me out." I then laid my hand on his forearm and looked directly into his eyes the way I had seen one of the characters, Charlotte I think her name is, on Sex and the City do. This move seemed to work for her and got her whatever she wanted; it must have worked for me too because he apologized and he seemed like he meant it.

I leaned over and kissed him and said, "Only think of me that way." I grinned and so did he. Now, I know I have already stated that I wasn't really into him and that we weren't a couple or anything, but that's one of the twisted things about life. Just because you don't really want something with someone doesn't mean you want him to think about or be with someone else either. I think it's psychological. You want to know that if you did decide to want something beyond what you have, that it would be possible, that there would be

no one else to compete with, that the two of you have something unique. Anyway, that's how I felt about Timothy, but
hell, I would never tell him that.

We started to hear moaning and the bed squeaking in
the other room. Guess they were done fighting. Timothy
giggled, almost like a little girl would. I think he was still
nervous. I was tempted to shut and lock my door and go
at it with him right there. I mean, if they think they are the
only ones who can do that whenever they please and forget about everyone else in the house, well, they've got a
rude awakening coming. But, I wasn't really horny and I
think Timothy was probably too nervous to make it enjoy-
able, so I said, "If you don't want to stay here and listen to
this, we could go out for ice cream. I'll buy."

Timothy glanced at me and then looked away. I briefly
wondered if he was going to say that he'd rather stay here
and listen. Gross! So, I grabbed his hand, pulled him off the
chair and said, "Come on."

I yelled, "We're going out for ice cream" as I passed their
door, but of course, I received no response and didn't expect
one. I knew it would be a long while before I saw them
again. I still had a hold of Timothy's hand when we reached
the front door, but I dropped it as we stepped outside. I
mean, I didn't want anyone to think we were a couple or
anything.

4

The next day, my mother started packing and harping at me to pack too. We still had two days before we were leaving and I couldn't see the point to starting now. In fact, I still needed to get that swimsuit. I actually thought of dragging Timothy to the store to help me pick out a suit, but then realized he would probably be comparing my scrawny, underdeveloped body to my mom's super curvy one. (The one that she said had caused the street signs "caution curves" to be made.) So, I decided against asking Timothy. I didn't really want to go by myself, but I didn't have any female friends to ask. Then I remembered Ethel. Even though she was old, she was the artistic type so I didn't think she'd be such a prude about high cut legs and stuff. I also knew she wouldn't make fun of my body or have nasty thoughts about my mother, especially since they had never met.

I made my usual morning trip to the museum, partly to see Ethel to check if she was free to shop and partly to get the hell away from my mother and her manic packing mode. She had packed and unpacked so many times, she would wear out her new luggage before it went anywhere. I mean, I know TravelPro has a lifetime warranty on their luggage, but they didn't know they would be up against my mom. She had enough new clothes and shoes shoved in there for a three-month trip and we were only planning to be gone a week. And she would pack, realize it wouldn't all fit, and then start yanking things out one by one and try them on again to see how they fit. And if I was there, she'd come ask me again…and again…and again what I thought of her new outfits. That's when I realized that the leopard print butt floss wasn't the only one. She'd bought g-strings and thongs in seven or eight colors. She said all of the hottest Hollywood people wore suits like that and that I should get one too.

I told her that the only people who wore those suits were Penthouse models, Brazilian beach bunnies, and sleazy strippers. My mother's response was, "Yeah, well some of them wish they had my body," and she actually stuck out her chest even more.

Then she said, "And speaking of Brazilian, I need to get a wax job again before we go. Why don't you come with me?"

I thought she'd finally lost her mind. Me, a sixteen-year-old, getting a wax job? What did she think I was, some chick on *The O.C.?* I barely even plucked my eyebrows, let alone wanted to pluck anything else.

"Come on. It'll be fun," she said. "We can go to the spa and get facials and manicures and pedicures. We'll make a whole day of it…tomorrow."

"I don't know," I hesitated. "The spa part sounds good, but…"

"Oh, come on. The wax is ripped off so quickly it only hurts for a sec. It will be fun. A great mother-daughter thing to do. Besides, I bet you could even do a drawing or a stencil of how you wanted your pubic hair done and they'd do it. They do all kinds of artistic things to it: dye it Tiffany blue, make it into a lightning bolt or a heart, or a landing strip. Then again, the Brazilian thing is to go hairless; that's what my suits call for."

I cringed. Information overload: that's what I was experiencing. "I don't know," I said again.

"Please," she said. Mom actually sounded like this meant a lot to her. I wavered, but finally decided it couldn't hurt to spend time with her, or at least it wouldn't hurt for long. I told her I'd go as long as I got to control what the wax lady did with the hair down there. She cheered and hugged me and said I wouldn't be sorry, that we'd do lunch too and just have the best time, like we used to. She made the appointments for 9 o'clock.

I left and went to the museum. I needed to see Ethel and get my fix in before I went to Maui. I loved that museum and didn't like the thought of being away from it for a whole week. Seven days. I hadn't been away from the museum for seven days since we'd moved here. The longest I ever stayed away was one day. I hoped it didn't change much while I was gone.

Ethel was finishing a church youth group tour. They were studying the Renoir statues, or at least they were supposed to be. A few kids in the back, they looked about 9 or 10, were jostling each other and poking each other and just goofing around. The sight disgusted me. No respect for the greatness whose presence they were in. Renoir was amazing, a genius, and these kids were uneducated, unappreciative assholes. And besides, they weren't paying Ethel any respect either. I skirted around the group and got behind the troublemakers. Thankfully, I was almost a head taller than them. I leaned between them and hissed, "God doesn't like your lack of respect and neither do I. Shut up and pay attention, asswipes." Their eyes grew large and round, but their mouths clamped shut. They stood rigid, almost at attention in military style. "That's better," I whispered and walked back a few paces so I could still see them but was no longer breathing down their scared, skinny necks.

Ethel finished up the presentation, thanked the kids for their attention, and then ushered them back to the entrance. I knew she had seen me and that she would be back so I stayed put and studied a painting from a new visiting exhibit. It was a piece called "Dinosaur" from some guy with an Irish sounding name. The painting was done in acrylics of tangerine, black, maroon, lemon yellow, slate blue, blue-charcoal, and lime green—an abstract. I thought it looked kind of amateurish and couldn't figure out where in the hell the title had come from. But then, every artist has a right to make what he or she wants or feels led to make, and this painting grew on me the longer I stared at it.

I heard the soft step of Ethel's Hush Puppies and turned. She looked lovely today in a flowing lavender button down tunic and long skirt that complemented her hair tint. Her blue eyes sparkled as she gently reached towards my hands. "Hello, dear. How are you today, Jessica?"

"I'm fine, Ethel. Quite a group you just had."

"Yes, there were some rambunctious ones. Thank you for taking care of those ones in the back. Their leaders didn't seem to do anything about it and they were like that the whole time."

I smiled and asked what time she finished work. She said she was actually just volunteering today, that she wasn't really on the schedule but had nothing much else to do. I told her I'd take her to lunch if she'd help me pick out a swimsuit.

"That was the thing I missed, just having a son," she said. "All those girl things, like swimsuit shopping and going to the beauty parlor together and to botanical gardens and teas and things." She had tears in her eyes. I remembered she had mentioned once that she did have a baby girl, many years ago, but she was stillborn. I reached for her hand and patted it. I also thought of my mom and our spa adventure tomorrow. I guess it was good that I said yes.

Shopping with Ethel was cool. She had an artistic eye just like mine so we seemed to gravitate towards the same types of things. My mom had given me cash, plus her department store credit cards, and I had some cash of my own. For once in my life, I decided to spend money, my own money, on clothes, not art supplies. I figured if I was going to Maui, I should look good. I just might meet a kindred spirit painting on the beach.

Ethel helped me pick out shorts and t-shirts and two bathing suits—bikinis that covered my ass and the chest I didn't really have. One was deep blue, like the Pacific Ocean. The other was a tasteful, but bright tropical floral, very Hawaiian. I had a blast shopping. Ethel made fun of the ugly clothes, but not loud and embarrassingly like my mother would have done. She used words like "interesting" and "unique" in her proper Southern accent, while holding the questionable item out in front of her so we'd both get a clear look at it. One such dress—a psychedelic, clingy polyester number got an "Interesting style and fabric choice" from her, with a smile on her face, and that sent me into fits of laughter. She laughed with me and remarked, "I don't know what some people are thinking when they design things. Must be designed by men, and straight ones at that, ones with no fashion-sense." I grinned and suppressed a giggle.

We moved on to Victoria's Secret to look at bras for me, A-cup of course. Ethel tried to talk me into the padded kind, saying the padding would give me a nice line under clothes. I tried to figure out a polite way to tell her I didn't believe in false advertising, but I knew that would open up a discussion about sex and my sex life in particular and I just wasn't comfortable enough to talk with her about that. I mean, she was cool and everything, but she was older and they did things differently in her day. Sixteen-year-olds may have had sex then, but usually because they were married. Well, maybe not at sixteen, but close to sixteen. Eventually, after trying on half a dozen styles, I compromised with Ethel and bought three bras that were shaped in the cup with a tiny layer of fiberfill, but that didn't have built-in boobs. I went with white for under t-shirts and tank tops, black because guys seem to like it, and a nude color one—boring but practical. I almost asked the girl behind the counter just who in the hell they fashioned the nude color bras after. None of them were ever skin color, at least not my skin color. They were always too dark or too taupe or too something; not even close to my pale shade. Anyway, I picked up some thongs and panties while Ethel had her back turned, looking at nightgowns and pantyhose. I didn't want her to know that much about me. And I know, I complain about my mom and her racy underwear, but I had to hand it to her; she knew a good thing when she found it. Thongs definitely gave you a better line, a smoother look in your clothing and if you bought one size bigger than your usual panty size, they were pretty damn comfortable. Plus, they felt kind of sexy.

Luckily, I didn't have to stand in line, as no customers were at the counter and the pantyhose and stuff kept Ethel busy. I checked out quickly, grabbed the bag, and led Ethel to Nordstrom's Café. I don't usually eat there, but have once or twice with Mom and remembered how many little old ladies were lunching at the time. I figured it'd be the perfect place for us, and besides they made a tasty barbeque chicken ranch salad.

As we got off the escalator, Ethel exclaimed, "Oh, I love this place. They have the best sandwiches and salads. And the cheesecake is good too. How about if we split a piece?" She beamed and didn't even look at the menu, just walked right up to the counter.

"Get whatever you want," I said. "I'm buying. Sure, I'll split cheesecake with you. Can we get it with strawberries?"

I paid while Ethel grabbed our number and went to find us a comfortable table where we could spread out a little with all of our packages. She had bought a dress and a pair of shoes so far and said she might go back for some of those Victoria's Secret pantyhose since they had control top. Did I know how they held up?

I told her I didn't since I hadn't worn pantyhose since my Wisconsin days. And back then I pretty much wore tights and not hose when I had to dress up in the cold winters, back when my stepfather was alive and made us go to church with him. The last time I was ever in a church was the morning he died. Mom wouldn't even hold his funeral service in the church, not that I think they would have let her, being a suicide and all, but she didn't even ask. I think she partly blamed the church—all the people and the pastor. She said he never felt he was good enough; he couldn't live up. I'm not quite sure what that means, but I am glad she doesn't make me sit through those boring services anymore.

Anyway, a man wearing a green apron approached with our food and hot teas on a tray. He took the plastic tented number off of our tabletop and replaced it with the food, placing a salad and a cup of tea before each of us (turns out my favorite salad is also Ethel's), and the cheesecake overflowing with perfect, ripe strawberries in between us with an extra plate.

"Oh, divine," Ethel said as she unfolded her napkin and placed it on her lap. "Thank you so much for today. It is so nice to get out of the museum and my condo and to be with a young person." She smiled at me and her blue eyes sparkled.

"Thanks," I said. "I appreciate all your help and couldn't have done this shopping trip without you. Shopping sucks, but you've made it fun." That was the truth. I would rather be home with my paints and my camera, creating my next masterpiece than spending time in this artificial, consumer-driven environment, but I was really enjoying my time with her. She had a dry but wicked sense of humor that I just loved.

After lunch, we decided to catch a movie, as I had nowhere to be and neither did she. There was an art house film place not too far from the mall and they were showing *Arsenic and Old Lace* from the 1940s with Cary Grant. It was one of my favorite old movies. Those two old ladies who kill old men and think they are doing a public service, or at least a service to the men and their loneliness, crack me up. And that guy who thinks he's Teddy Roosevelt and goes into the basement to dig graves for the "yellow fever victims" is a hoot too. What a loony!

I wasn't really in the mood for popcorn, since we had just eaten huge salads and cheesecake, but as Ethel said, "You can't go to the movies and not have popcorn," so we did. We got a small and split it. Ethel actually paid for the movies and munchies, plus two bottles of water. She said it was because I paid before, that it was only proper for her to pay now. I let her because it seemed to make her feel good to buy me something, plus I didn't want to infringe upon her Southern manners.

Both of us must have seen the movie a million times because we whispered "I just love this scene coming up" and "isn't this part great" throughout the hour and a half.

When the movie was over, Ethel took me straight home, and said, "I had a delightful day, dear, just delightful." She gave me a hug and told me she would see me tomorrow at the museum. I reminded her that I might not make it before closing since Mom and I were spending the day bonding at the spa.

"Give your mother credit, dear," Ethel said. "She loves you very much and wants to spend time with you. That's more than some mothers are able to do…spend time, you know." Her eyes glistened a little and I wondered if she was thinking of her baby daughter or of the high-powered son she rarely saw.

I thanked her for everything and headed into the house. If Mom was there, she'd make me model all the new stuff for her. I sort of hoped she wouldn't be, or at least that she and Jim would be otherwise occupied so they'd leave me alone. I really needed to paint as I hadn't done anything creative at all for almost 24 hours. I know that some people believe in the use-it-or-lose-it philosophy; I never adopted that one. The reason I paint or draw or do some other type of artistic endeavor every day is because of the hole. I feel this huge, gaping hole inside. The only way it even begins to feel full is by expressing myself through some creative outlet. Some people use drugs. Unless the oil paint odor makes me high, I don't believe in mind-altering narcotics. I believe in expression, in getting to a higher level—or consciousness or whatever—through colors and textures and words, and in some cases, sounds. All I know is that what is in me every day must come out or maybe that what is in me mentally has to pass through a canvas or a camera or something to go back into me, in my spirit, for me to feel like I have successfully spent the day. And each day, a little of that hole gets filled—as long as I paint.

Anyway, I got my wish. When I walked into the house, there was a note on the fridge that said if I hadn't eaten, some Healthy Choice dinners were in the freezer. It also said she and Jim were not to be disturbed.

Like I'd even consider that.

I was able to get in a great night of painting. I worked a little more, adding some highlights, to my impressionistic piece of Timothy. You know, he really isn't half bad. I mean, he's kind of uncool at school, not popular, I mean, but he's really nice. Plus, he pays attention to me when I want some. Attention, I mean…but sex too, and he's not so bad at that either.

After I finished that painting to my liking, I started a new oil on a 20-by-24 stretched canvas. I just love oils because you can blend them and texturize them over time, making your masterpiece always incomplete until you are done with it. Kind of reminds me of people. We aren't done shaping our personalities and our lives until we are dead. The slow dry-rate of oils makes them the same way: shapeable.

Anyway, I painted the entire canvas black, straight out of the tube black. The paint was far from flat though. The lights caught the oil and the black shimmered. I added to that a swirl of phthalo green and a zigzag of permanent rose and a swoosh of phthalo blue, once again all straight from the tube. It needed yellow, cadmium yellow, so I painted a soft circle of yellow in the upper left corner. I added a cadmium orange triangle to the bottom right corner, and some kind of funky trapezoid in dioxazine purple to the upper right corner. I grabbed tubes then, without thought to the color and just added different shapes, and almost shapes, to the painting in a blind fury. One tube after another tube, after another, never cleaning my brush between. My painting was bright—like the sky lit with neon. It was wild and uninhibited and crazy. And it was full of movement, movement that seemed to transcend the canvas, to transcend time and space. I loved it!

After my fury had passed, I possessed a sense of finality. That the painting was over, or at least the creation of it was. I was exhausted; the birth of great art is painful and I seemed to outdo myself once again. That's the thing about my art. I am not really trying to compete against other artists; I compete only against myself. Each painting, each piece of art has to show growth, more emotion, more *something* than the last piece, as I am an evolving creature. We are an evolving species.

I plopped my brushes into their bath, moved the easel so it sat at the foot of my bed. I wanted to be able to see the new painting with the first rays of light in the morning. I was too tired to even wash my face so I just stripped and crawled between the sheets. I fell asleep as soon as my head hit the pillow.

The next morning, I remembered having the weirdest dream. It involved snakes that kept crawling on me and wouldn't get off. No matter how hard I pushed them, or even when I picked them up and tried to throw them, they wouldn't leave me alone. They clung to me. It didn't make sense. Snakes have no arms and can't cling to anything, but that's what the snakes in my dream did.

Part of me wanted to paint it as a way of exorcising the dream. Another part of me wanted nothing to do with it, not to remember it and certainly not to make it live eternally on canvas. I tried to put it out of my head.

Jim was already gone when I scurried from my room to the bathroom to take a shower. Mom was in the kitchen singing along to Jennifer Lopez on the radio. She must have made coffee because I could smell it. And I swear I heard her feet dancing. It was too early for that.

I ran the water extra hot, thinking it might wash the dream away. It didn't.

After I got out of the shower, I ran a comb through my stringy hair and put some Neosporin on my wrist scars, hoping the ointment would help them diminish. That was a shameful, secretive time in my short history. Then I wrapped a towel around my middle and scooted to my room. On the way there, I heard my mother remind me to forgo makeup since we were getting facials in an hour. Like I ever wear much makeup in the first place. But *what*ever.

I looked out the window and realized that the day was actually overcast — not just smoggy — rare around here. Mom yelled down the hall asking if I wanted breakfast, that she was making a fruit smoothie, and did I want one. That was her idea of breakfast. I yelled back, "No" and that I'd eat a banana and toast when I came out, and to save some coffee for me. I needed the caffeine jumpstart. I think that dream made me more tired. Is that even possible?

I put on a t-shirt, shorts, and sandals since we'd change into those plush white Turkish robes at the spa. I put my hair back in a ponytail, pulled up the sheet and comforter on my bed so I could pretend it was made, and then gazed lovingly at my creation from last night. It looked even more splendid in the natural light of day. The thought of showing it to Mom passed through my brain and was instantly rejected. I already knew what she'd say. So, I just smiled at the painting one last time then left my room and headed to the kitchen.

Mom was still dancing—I wished she wasn't—but this time it was to a Madonna tune. She really could dance. Mom, I mean. Well, Madonna could too, but she was a little too pop culture for me. I preferred to listen to singers and groups who weren't really famous, ones who were strug-gling like me, or at least ones who weren't legends in their own time. Groups like Letters to Cleo and Semisonic and singers like Andru Donalds.

If art wasn't where my gifts were, I'd probably have tried my hand at singing, or maybe acting. I have a good voice, or at least close to perfect pitch, that I inherited from my mom. She could sing and in fact used to. She tells stories, embarrassing ones usually, about being a nightclub singer while she was in college, says that's how she paid tuition and that's also where she met my dad. I guess it could have been worse: she could've been a stripper or something. The way she loves her body, I'm surprised she wasn't.

But anyway. My dad. I haven't mentioned him as of yet. That's because I never knew him. She said he was some married guy who used to come hear her sing, that he broke her heart, and she never told him about me. I guess it's true, or at least I have no reason not to believe it.

That's what I thought about as I ate my breakfast and drank a cup of really strong coffee—black with sugar. Espresso it probably was. I loved the way cream mixed into coffee; the way it swirled and then created a new color or shade when it was mixed. But, the stuff screws up my sinuses and makes me all snuffily and drippy. Really plays havoc with those mucus membranes, so I abstained.

As soon as I finished and stuck my spoon, plate, and cup in the dishwasher, Mom was rushing me to go, saying the freeway would be busy. I said we couldn't leave until I brushed my teeth. I didn't want to end up with a mouth full of metal like her. She has so many of those silver fillings from when she was a kid. She has started to get them replaced with the clear fillings, because now it is being debated if the metal ones are harmful. Hasn't harmed her any, at least that we can tell.

Mom was right about the freeway: bumper-to-bumper. Must have been an accident. We left the house with plenty of time and ended up arriving right on time.

Raquel, the owner of the spa, and my mother are on a first name basis; my mom goes there so often. Raquel personally escorted us to the back where the changing rooms are. She handed each of us a cedar hanger and an Asian silk pouch for jewelry, which I wasn't wearing. Mom said the rooms were big enough we could change together. I cringed. I didn't want to see my mother's naked body again. Once during the week was plenty, let alone twice in a 72-hour time period. But, I didn't argue and just kept my eyes on the floor and walls.

The robes and slippers were the softest and fluffiest I have ever felt. And the robe smelled so good, like roses. When I buried myself deeper into the oversized robe and closed my eyes, I could see them. Bright yellow, vivid magenta, deep lavender, creamy white, carmine red roses with dark green leaves and stems. God, my mind was seeing in brilliant colors lately. I breathed deeply. The aroma was heavenly.

Mom opened the door to the dressing room and I followed her out. Raquel handed me over to a girl named Melinda who couldn't have been all that much older than me. Or, I guess she was since she had skin care training, but she looked young. She had coppery hair with ringlets every which way, not like Medusa, but like a red-headed, older Shirley Temple. And she had faint freckles and flawless skin, a bi-product of where she worked, I guessed. Can't have a pimply skin care worker, bad for business. I smiled at the thought.

She had me lay on what looked suspiciously like a massage table covered in a sheet topped by a cocoon of blankets.

Melinda wrapped the blanket and sheets around me so I was mummified. She said it was important to feel warm, like I was in the womb, that I would relax better and so would my skin.

Whatever.

Mom was on a similar table across the room.

I closed my eyes and just focused on all the bright colors I saw in my head. I could feel the heat of a bright light over my face and Melinda said I had beautiful skin, but a few clogged pores. I murmured agreement, figuring that happened when I created the masterpiece with my mom's makeup. I said nothing else, as I really didn't want to get all chummy with her. The warm liquid she was putting on my face felt great, sort of comforting. I was starting to be glad Mom suggested this…and was willing to pay for it. I took a deep, cleansing breath and just let Melinda work her magic. I concentrated on the shapes taking place in my brain, on thinking about my next project. Occasionally, one of those damn snakes crossed my visual memory. Actually, this time they looked more like eels all electrified or glowing. Weird. Once Timothy's face came to mind, and once Jim's face fleeted passed, but for some reason the image that stuck was hands, the same ones from my painting, the ones that could have belonged to Jim. That made me snap my eyes open, dangerously, since that luminescent bulb was right over my face.

I had no idea of my facial expression but it must have changed from its serenity because Melinda asked if I was okay, did I want a drink of water or tea or something. She said she thought I was asleep. I said, "No, daydreaming," but "daymaring" was more accurate. Melinda told me to take ten deep breaths and she massaged my temples, trying to help me return to my relaxed state. I could hear my mother snoring, but blocked it out. I forced myself to think of Ethel and our fun yesterday and willed myself to think happy thoughts. I know it sounds corny, but I find it works. So, I concentrated on paints and sand and waves and beach balls and Maui, since we'd be leaving in a little over 24 hours.

When my face was properly scrubbed, facialized, moisturized and whatever the hell else Melinda did to clean my pores and make my skin radiant, she led me to someone else, a massage therapist. Mom was already there on the table next to the one that was to be mine. "Hi, honey," she said. "Having fun?"

"Sure. Thanks," I said. Some larger woman with an unrecognizable foreign accent asked me to disrobe and put a sheet around me. I climbed back up on the table and lay on my front side as instructed, while she rubbed some kind of lotion or oil between her hands and then poured the chilly stuff on me. I wriggled a little, involuntarily. She was surprisingly gentle, but firm, and really worked my muscles. And she wasn't one for conversation, not that I could with my mouth mooshed into the table. The only thing she said was "You are very tense for your age, no?"

I hadn't ever thought about it, but of course, that was just what I did for the rest of the session.

After that, I re-robed and was led, with Mom, to the pedicure ladies. Mine was a very petite Asian—Thai, I think—with gorgeous, shiny long hair. I'd kill for hair like that. Well, okay, not really kill, but you know what I mean. She plopped my callused feet into a soaking bath that wafted a light eucalyptus scent. She then disappeared and reappeared quickly with a bone china teacup brimming with an herbal brew. Raquel appeared then and said, "Oh, good. That is my special house blend: raspberry lemon tea."

I took a sip to be polite and then took another because it was fabulous. "Delicious," I declared.

Mom said, "Raquel, it's splendid as always." Then they started gossiping about someone they both seemed to know and whether or not he was still with someone they referred to as "the bitch" and what he could have possibly seen in her. I tried to tune them out.

The tea really was good. I wondered if Raquel shared recipes or even sold the stuff. I'd have to ask.

My feet felt the beginnings of a shrivel and the pedicurist seemed to sense the same because she grabbed a fluffy white towel (could have matched the robe) and took a foot at a time out of the bath. She gently patted my skin, treating it better than I ever have and then she put the dry foot back into my slipper and worked on the other one. She filed and clipped my toenails, pumiced the rough spots on my heels and the backs of my big toes, and then had me select a polish. I chose hot pink and asked if she'd do my fingernails in the same color, when the time came.

After my feet, they had me stay put to do my hands. First, we paraffin dipped and wrapped from the wrist down in Saran Wrap and put my hands into what looked like oven mitts. Then, we got our manicures. My hands were sort of a mess before we started, which the Asian lady was quick to point out. The oil paints bleed into your fingerprint ridges. It's hell to get out and I had given up trying. Surprisingly, the antiseptic wash they gave me before the paraffin actually removed a lot of that embedded paint. My hands hadn't been this clean in years.

After a light lunch of salad and breadsticks, served by the

spa staff, came the part I was dreading: the bikini torture. Mom was excited as they led us into yet another room. "Oh, Jessica, now you are really a woman. Your first bikini wax." I stared at her. I thought having sex made me a woman not having some strange woman pull out my pubes. I almost said so, but Mom was on to something else. She was rambling to the waxer about how it was my first time and how she should be gentle and how she told me that I could choose any design I wanted, or make my hair any color.

The waxer, a female in her 20s with a buzz cut, looked happy. Too happy for her job, or maybe she liked to torture people in this way. She made me lay on the table on my back. God, this place had so many tables. The spa was huge. She asked me my name and said hers was T.C. I told her that was an interesting name.

"Yeah," she said. "They actually named me Teresa Charlotta, but do I look like a Teresa to you? Mother Teresa I ain't." I smiled at that. Good point. Mother Teresa wouldn't work in L.A. making women hairless, or nearly that, in their nether regions.

"So, do you want a design?" she asked, spreading my legs and lifting my robe. I could see my wiry, blond hairs. They probably looked all scraggly and unkempt to her. Luckily, Mom wasn't watching and was on a table at the far end of the room with one of her own legs in the air and too much of her exposed. I turned my head and looked the other way.

"I don't know," I said, still not sure about any of this.

"Sure, something to surprise the boyfriend with? You got a boyfriend or significant other or someone?" T.C. looked me full in the face. Her hand was on my leg, but in a non-sexual way, which was good considering how exposed and uncomfortable I felt.

"Uh…" I didn't want Mom to hear. "Sort of," I whispered.

"Well, what'd you think he'd like? Or is it a she? Can't be too certain nowadays." She grinned.

Yeah, I thought. I'd bet you'd prefer the latter. "I don't care what he'd like," I said softly. "What do you usually do?"

"Well, we can do the basic: remove the hair from the sides, the bikini line area. Or, we can make it shorter, meaning start lower and do the sides, you know, like a landing strip."

My insides felt all squirmy. I didn't want to be talking about this. "Uh, okay, yeah. Do that." I wanted to get this over with as soon as possible. This was humiliating.

She forced my leg straight up and out to the side slightly and then applied some warm goo to the inside of my leg. Then she put some kind of cloth strip over that and said, "On the count of three, now."

I held my breath and she pulled, or was it ripped? It hurt like hell, but then subsided almost as fast.

She showed me the strip. All these squiggly hairs were stuck to it. It looked cool and artistic. I smiled.

"See. Not so bad," she said and applied something that felt like rubbing alcohol to the now-bald area. "Now for the other side."

This side was much better for me as I knew what to expect. I was starting to get into it and asked if she could do some on the top and maybe trim a little. Maybe we could color it too. That might be fun. Or a smiley face. We could dye it yellow and maybe put black eyes and a smiley in raven hair dye on what hair I had left. It'd be cool for shock value. At least to shock Timothy with. I didn't tell him I was coming here; it was too embarrassing. But at least now I could surprise him. I mean, this waxing business was making me feel sexy, making me want to get laid.

I smiled and let T.C. wax her magic.

6

Mom had a surprise for me when I got done with T.C. She said that Raquel was able to get us appointments at one of L.A.'s hippest salons, so we were heading there to get our hair done. "Can't let the hair on our heads look all scraggily while the rest of us looks fabulous," she said.

I rolled my eyes but smiled. This spending time with Mom wasn't half bad, at least because we weren't really together and I didn't run into anyone I knew. And the chick at the salon did a great job on my hair, not that my stringy, thin bird's nest was ever going to resemble Mom's shiny, thick tresses. But at least now my hair had some bounce and the split ends had been snipped. My hair wore more styling products than I used in a year, but the blonde looked shinier and it was blown out in a Heather Locklear kind of way. I looked pretty damn good, I thought. And I felt fairly sexy.

Mom wanted to go to the gym on the way home. I told her I'd pass, just to drop me off at the museum and I'd take the bus home. The security guard at the front desk, old, chubby, gray-haired Joe, took his hat off to me and said, "Afternoon, Jessica. You are looking fine today. Did you get a new hairdo?" He actually dipped a little like a bow and held the door for me.

"Thanks, Joe," I said and beamed my biggest smile. It felt good to be noticed.

A few other museum employees complimented me on my hair as I walked past them. I thanked each one and wandered through the building, searching for Ethel. Maybe she wasn't there. I stopped in front of the new exhibit, the one with that Dinosaur painting. I walked from right to left and left to right, slowly, taking in each painting from different angles. A couple of them were mesmerizing, such intense design and color, such strong emotion. I could almost feel what the artist must have felt during the creation process. One painting felt heavy and sad, while the next in the series felt lighter, but still sorrowful. The one at the end had a completely different tone and color scheme, almost like it didn't fit in the series. I wondered what had caused the change, not just in the painting, but in the painter. This acrylic piece seemed almost happy, not elated, but definitely had twinges of joy. Well, that was as good a one as any, I thought, at least to stop on for the day.

I checked in at the desk and found out Ethel had called in sick. That was weird. I hoped she was okay. I didn't know exactly where she lived, so I couldn't go check on her, but I'd look it up in the book when I got home and try to call.

When I got home, I found Ethel wasn't listed. Jim wasn't home and neither was Mom. I decided to start packing since we were leaving tomorrow afternoon. I lugged my rolling suitcase out from under the bed. I made piles of underwear, bras, tanks, shorts, etc., all over the bed. Then I picked out some of my older brushes, still useable. I wanted older ones in case my luggage got lost and was never found. Didn't want to risk my newer, better brushes. They were damned expensive.

After I got all that squared away, I looked in the mirror one more time. I did look good, or at least the best I ever had, not that I would ever win a beauty pageant or anything. I added a touch of mascara, some blush to my pale cheeks, and a little bit of lip gloss and a short spritz of perfume, a very light one, one of those unisex kinds from Calvin Klein. I liked what I saw.

I ran next door, knowing Timothy's mom would be at work. She was a nurse and worked weird shifts, but she was on the late one this week. I tapped softly on the door as he opened it. He must have been waiting since I came home, probably saw me walking up the street.

"Wow!" he said.

I pushed him back as I wanted to get through the door with no one seeing me. Not that we had nosy neighbors, but you can never be too safe. He encircled the wrist of my hand that was pushing him, and drew me closer, a lot closer, actually against him. I probably would have fallen if it wasn't for his wall of a body holding me up. He kissed me deeply. I felt his tongue at the back of my throat, roaming around my mouth, inspecting my teeth. He wasn't usually this passionate. And if the haircut had caused this, wait until he saw the other surprises.

He pulled away and leaned back a little. My turn to say, "Wow." I'd never been kissed like that before, by anyone.

"You are so hot," he said with a major grin on his face. He looked me up and down. "Come 'ere." He clasped my hand and led me to his room. I had never been there before, as we usually did it at my house, or once in the woods behind his old elementary school. His room was kind of boyish, I guess. Blue carpet and green bedspread, bed made. A couple of posters on the wall—one of Bill Gates, another of some scantily clad bimbo leaning over a Ferrari, a third of the latest Star Wars movie. Model cars and planes on one shelf, books on another. Huge computer set up on a large wooden desk that probably belonged in an office, not some kid's bedroom. A TV, 25-inch at least, sat in the corner on a stand with some video games and a console under it, plus a DVD player and scads of discs. I swear he owned more movies than I'd ever seen, or at least the piles stacked in the corner made it look that way.

He led me to the bed and told me to sit. He walked to a cabinet in the corner and opened it to expose a rockin' stereo. I guessed being a sort-of nerd had its advantages: he sure knew how to build a good sound system. He put on some group I had never heard of, but they sounded okay. He shut the blinds so that it was fairly dark. Then he said he'd be back and disappeared out the door.

I stretched out on the bed, smiling as I thought about the trip to the spa. Timothy returned quickly with something balled into his fist. He opened his nightstand drawer. I was tempted to look and see what he had in there, but I didn't want to be nosy. Turned out it was candles, lots of the them. He put them around the room and lit them one by one. The glow cast warm shadows around the room and was so romantic. He was so sweet and had obviously put some thought into this. I wondered how he knew I'd come today or if he had just been waiting, holding onto this stuff in case it ever happened.

He shut his bedroom door and walked toward the bed. He was gazing at me, his face intense, but unreadable. He crawled across the bedspread so that he lay next to me, stretched out with his body lightly touching mine. He outlined my face and then my lips with his finger. And then he kissed me again, gently at first and then deeply, like he did in the doorway. I felt a tingle between my legs and knew that I wanted him badly. I tried to roll on top of him.

He gently pushed me and said, "Slowly. We have time. You're always in such a rush." He kissed me lightly on the lips. "We've got time."

I couldn't believe it: since when was he in charge? But he had obviously gone to a lot of trouble. He was right; I didn't have anywhere to go, nothing to do but him. It wouldn't hurt me to just wait and see what happened. I let him lead.

When we got to the part, actually almost a half an hour later, where he was taking off my pants and thong, he gasped. "When did you do this?" he asked.

"Do you like it?" I tried to look all innocent, with wide eyes, slightly raised eyebrows, and a little smile.

"I've never seen anything like it." His fingers caressed the little bit of fuzz I had left.

"Never? Not even in those trashy magazines you guys read?" I joked and squirmed slightly. He was tickling me with his caress.

"Who, me? I don't read trashy magazines unless you consider *Red Herring* and *Newsweek* trashy."

"What? No *Maxim* or *Stuff* or *Playboy?*" He blushed so I knew I was on to something. I licked his chin with the tip of my tongue and then licked his bottom lip. He smashed his lips against mine so I knew I had him. We kissed while I

worked my fingers feverishly trying to get his pants unbut-
toned, unzipped, and down. I was completely naked and he
wasn't. It wasn't fair.

At one point, Timothy, now naked, stopped kissing me
and running his hands up and down my body. He slid down
my body and did something I have only seen in movies, you
know, that thing Kevin did to Tara Reid's character in
American Pie. I was freaked out at first, but it felt really good
really fast and I couldn't catch my breath enough to complain. I don't know what came over Timothy, but I liked it.
As long as he didn't expect me to return that favor. That was
something I didn't do, something that brought back bad
memories.

I just closed my eyes and concentrated on how it felt, and
at some point, I heard him open the condom wrapper. Then
he entered me and started pumping away and I didn't care
anymore about anything.

Later, he talked me into staying, staying overnight that is.
Said his mom was working a double shift and wouldn't be
home until seven. I figured, what the hell, I wouldn't be
seeing him for a week. I peeked through the blinds to see
who was home at my house. Both of their cars were in the
driveway, but the house was all dark. Mom was probably
introducing Jim to her new wax job. They wouldn't even
notice I was gone, so I agreed. "Let me just run next door
and grab a toothbrush," I said.

He reached into his nightstand and pulled out a red one,
with hearts on the handle. "Here, this is for you," he said, and
looked kind of embarrassed.

I paused. What the hell was going on? We weren't a
couple. He shouldn't be doing this shit. He actually seemed

like he was falling for me. We were just supposed to be friends, friends with benefits. I grabbed the toothbrush and mumbled "thanks" and hurried into the bathroom. I locked the door behind me and sat on the toilet. Tears streamed down my cheeks, but I couldn't have told you why. I sobbed. I sobbed so hard I got the hiccups.

I heard Timothy at the door, asking if I was all right. "Yeah," I choked, hoping he heard me, but that he couldn't tell I was crying. "I'm going to take a quick shower." I ran the water. At least that would give me an excuse for having a wet face.

"The towels on the rack are clean," he said through the door. I heard him walk away.

I took a deep breath and climbed in under the hot water. I was still crying but the sobs had subsided, along with the squeaky little hiccup noise. *Pull yourself together, girl, I said to myself. It's been a perfect day. You were pampered and coddled and got along with Mom. Plus, you had some of the best sex of your life. Get over it, whatever it is. Life is good, even if you didn't get to paint.*

Paint. Maybe that was it. But I honestly didn't feel the need at that moment. I couldn't feel the hole or it felt filled or something. I didn't understand; all I knew was that for once, I didn't feel so empty.

When I stepped out of the bathroom with the towel wrapped around my middle, I heard Timothy yell, "I'm in the kitchen, but I put my robe on the bed for you, if you want it. It's clean." Tears sprung to my eyes again, but I blinked until they went away.

"Thanks," I said so softly he probably hadn't heard. I padded into his room, slipped on his robe, which was surprisingly cozy, and found my way to the kitchen.

"Hey, I thought you'd be hungry. Hope spaghetti is okay. I can't make much else."

I chuckled at that because that summed up my culinary skills, too. Spaghetti, frozen food, toast, canned soup, macaroni and cheese, and packaged salad—it's what we lived off of at my house. "Move over, I'll stir the sauce," I said. My God, I thought, this is as close to Pleasantville as I'll ever get.

Timothy walked over to a kitchen cabinet and pulled out a bottle of wine. "Red goes with red sauce, right?"

"Uhhh…sure," I said. How the hell would I know? He opened the bottle rather expertly and filled two stemmed glasses half full. I held mine to the light. The stemware was lead crystal, and it sparkled and showed colors under the kitchen ceiling lights. It was beautiful: the glass, the liquid, such an iridescent purple. It looked like art.

I swallowed a sip and then splashed some into the sauce. I had seen Emeril do that on TV once. Timothy was just standing there, staring at me.

"What?" I asked, feeling self-conscious.

"You are so beautiful," he said.

"Don't."

"But you are."

"I said, 'don't'. You're embarrassing me." I turned away from him and concentrated on the red, hot sauce that was starting to bubble.

"I can't help it," he said. "And I don't mean to embarrass you. I just don't think you know how beautiful you are."

That was it. The tears fell and I ran from the room.

"Jessica, I'm sorry." He was coming after me.

"The sauce is going to burn," I said.

"The hell with the sauce," he said. "Talk to me. What's wrong?"

"Just go back to the kitchen. I'm fine." I tried to push him away, but instead, he wrapped his arms around me and held me tight. He murmured, "It's okay" and "shush" as I cried. I would have paid a million dollars to be able to stop. But I couldn't. I felt like my insides were leaking out and that they wouldn't stop until there was nothing left. I didn't even fight him anymore.

He lay with me on the bed, trying to comfort me. I couldn't talk, couldn't do anything but cry.

And then finally, I stopped, just like someone had turned off the spigot. I don't know how much time had passed, how much time I spent sobbing. I was sure dinner was ruined.

He pulled back a little and looked at my puffy, wet face. Quietly he said, "Are you okay?"

I managed a weak smile and said, "Sure, I'll be fine. Now we need to eat."

He seemed to take that as a sign that I didn't want to talk about it because he got up, handed me a box of Kleenex, and then took off for the kitchen to try and salvage dinner.

I wiped off my face and then realized I was cold because the hot tears all over the robe were cooling. I opened Timothy's closet and nosed around, searching for a sweatshirt. I found one that said "Stanford" on the chest and figured he was smart enough to go there someday. I disrobed and slipped it over my head. I grabbed a pair of his flannel boxers out of a drawer and hoped he wouldn't mind. Actually, in his oversized clothes, I thought I looked kind of cute. I just hoped he wouldn't get the wrong idea.

After splashing water on my face, I re-entered the kitchen. He smiled when he saw what I was wearing, but said nothing except, "Dinner's hosed. Your choices are frozen pizza or microwave popcorn. Or we could just finish the wine."

"Pizza's fine. I can make it. I know how," I said. He was already soaking the burnt spaghetti and scorched sauce pans. I was exhausted. All that crying and sex was getting to me. I hoped I could stay awake to eat. He must have been as tired as me because he yawned and said while the pizza cooked, he would take a shower.

So, I stood in the kitchen watching the pizza, unable to think of anything better to do. The cheese fascinated me, or at least the cooking and melting of the cheese fascinated me. Have you ever studied a cooking pizza? When it goes into the oven, it's all frozen and hard and the cheese is all grated and piled like a bunch of ecru worms. Then, as it starts to thaw, the outer edges of the crust turn from that pale beige color to a toasty brown and the cheese starts to move, actually looks like it's sliding, as it melts. And parts of it start to bubble, just around the edges. The pieces of cheese that are stuck to the crust, away from the other cheese, get dried out somehow and turn a crispy brown, a darker brown than the crust—sort of like burnt umber to raw umber. A cooking pizza could be classified as "performance art." It's amazing.

When Timothy emerged from his shower, he was dressed in a twin outfit to mine. Oh great! Twinks, I thought. At least no one else would see us. I told him the pizza was almost done and he grabbed a bag of salad out of the fridge, dumped half in each bowl on the counter and asked what kind of dressing I preferred, saying they had Catalina, Ranch, and Italian. French was my favorite so I chose the first one. "Just a little, though," I said. "I hate swimming lettuce."

He smiled and made two identical salads. I wasn't sure if

that was his choice or if he was again trying to be like me. Made me wonder. I didn't need a twin. Just needed some guy to keep his mouth shut and to screw occasionally. A fuck puppet, that's what I needed, and the thought made me grin.

We ate, watched some B-movies on TV, cleaned up the dishes, and just relaxed. Around one, he suggested we go back to bed since we only had six more hours to ourselves. I didn't want his mom to find me there. He kept saying that it was cool, that she wouldn't care, but that was too much.

When we got back to his room, we didn't sleep. First of all, it was hard to get comfortable on his twin bed, at least comfortable enough to sleep. So, instead of sleeping, we went at it again…and again, until it was almost time for his mom to come home. I snuck back into my own house. Mom and Jim were still in their room with the door shut. I should have been tired after all that crying and not sleeping, but instead I felt inspired. Maybe it was Timothy and the new things he did to me, maybe it was the creativity of the pizza cheese, but whatever it was didn't matter. I knew I had to paint. And that is what I did in a feverish, haphazard man-ner. I slapped color on canvas and just let the muse work through me. I let whatever was going to transpire take place. Exhaustion overpowered me around 9 A.M. and I slept. At least until noon, when my mother started banging on my door asking what the hell I was doing. We had to leave for the airport in 20 minutes. Luckily, I was already packed.

I took a two-minute shower, towel dried my hair, dressed, wrapped a painting in freezer paper, and ran next door. I didn't need to knock; apparently, Timothy saw me coming, as he opened the door and whispered, "My mother is sleeping."

"Here," I said, handing him the package. "This is for you. Thanks for last night." And then I turned and ran back to my house before he could say anything.

7

The flight to Maui wasn't bad. Though I sometimes can't stand the fact that he took Mom away from me, Jim could be a really nice guy. He surprised us and used his frequent flier miles to upgrade the three of us to first class. They sat in the first row and I sat in the last, next to an empty seat. That was fine by me. I leaned against the window and slept most of the time. I awoke to choose my meal and then to eat it on a real plate with real utensils, sans knife. That surprised me. I had never flown first class before so I didn't know I wouldn't have to use the plastic crap…and that I'd have a choice for my entrée. Pretty cool. I chose the salmon with the mango chutney, mainly because the other options were pasta (which reminded me too much of last night) and filet mignon—which I didn't trust to airline chefs. Plus, I don't eat much red meat. So, the salmon seemed the safest, and it really wasn't half bad. It came with a salad with balsamic dressing—not my favorite, but I had no choice—, a hard roll with butter (the real stuff, not that fake margarine, oily stuff), and a side of rice pilaf. The healthiest meal I'd eaten in a while. Afterward, the flight attendant came around with a coffee and tea service and homemade brownie sundaes, and by homemade I mean she made them up at the front of the cabin to passenger specifications.

On a full stomach, I curled up happily and went back to sleep. I could have watched a movie, but I wasn't really interested in the selections. And besides, sleep is good.

I awoke as we landed in Kahului. Getting our luggage went fairly quickly, at least faster than I have experienced with the luggage carousels at LAX. Those luggage handlers seem to take forever. While Mom and I waited for the luggage, Jim went to get the car. He had rented a Jeep—an honest, rough type of Jeep, not the Cherokee. I think this one was called a Wrangler. I couldn't imagine why he didn't want something that rode smoother, more luxuriously, like his Porsche. God, that 4-wheel-drive tin can was bumpy; it made you feel every groove in the road. But Jim just smiled and said Maui was the place for fun and the vehicle was fun. I prayed I wouldn't get sunburned on the way to the hotel—a long 45 minutes from the airport.

The hotel was awesome, right on the beach, Kaanapali Beach to be exact. I had never seen anything like it, or at least I hadn't stayed in anything like it. I hadn't traveled much. Jim had booked us two, oceanfront rooms—connecting ones—at the Hyatt Regency Resort and Spa. It was fabulous with lush foliage all around, a wacky freeform pool that was over a half-acre in size, tennis courts (not that I played), a waterfall Jacuzzi, and so much more. I dumped my stuff in my room and told them I was headed out to explore. No one objected so I went right ahead.

I visited every floor in each of the three towers to see if

they looked any different from one another, and to see if the snack machines were different, in case I got the munchies. Then I perused the lobby-level shops—very expensive stuff in those—and visited the videogame arcade, where I played nothing, but saw a bunch of little boys and a couple of adult men who thought they were still little boys.

Outside, I wandered around the pool and the bar and finally sat in a chair with a sigh. I was in Hawaii, the most exotic place I'd ever been. The weather was great, but not that much different from L.A. Only an older couple was in the pool, and a family with a toddler was splashing further down. Life was good.

But I was going to get one hell of a sunburn if I didn't apply sunscreen and change into a different shirt, and maybe my floppy sun hat—not very chic, but it does the job. See, my skin does two things: burns slightly and fries. I do not have shades of beige like some people; I go from pasty white to pink and then to blistery lobster. And it's not much fun so I take precautions—as uncool as it may be. I'll never be a beach bunny.

So, I took the elevator up to my room. Entering, I stopped dead in my tracks. Sitting on the dresser was a fairly large basket, wrapped with a bow, and filled with art supplies and canvas. There was a gift card sticking out of the top. I opened the envelope and peered inside to see, in a hand-writing I didn't recognize, "For your stay here. Enjoy! Love, Jim." Wow! First class plane tickets and a lot of paints. Maybe this thing he had with my mother wasn't so bad. Sure, I felt left out at times, but who the hell cared? I was swimming in paints!

I banged on the connecting door and yelled, "Mom! Jim!"

She opened the door, dressed solely in her butt floss. Her top was in her hand. I tried not to cringe. "What?"

"I just wanted to thank you and Jim for the art supplies. You're the best." I gave her a hug.

"Art supplies?" She stepped into my room. "Oh, you're welcome. Glad you like them." The way she was looking at them told me she knew nothing about them.

"Well, I'm getting ready to head to the beach. Did you want to come?" She put on her bikini top and adjusted it to its proper position.

"Ummm. Probably not. I don't want to get fried my first day here. Where's Jim?" He obviously wasn't in their room.

"He went off to look at some properties. Said he didn't need our input yet. I'll tell him you said thanks for the paints. There sure are a lot of them." She stared at the basket.

"Yes. I'm thankful, can't wait to use them. I'm gonna look at the book on the table, the one that tells you what to see on the island. I read on the Internet that some park is the best place to watch the sunrise, but you have to go at three in the morning. I might do that tomorrow." I realized I was rambling because I was nervous. I didn't like the way she was looking at the basket. "Do you want to come?"

She looked me square in the face. "At three o'clock in the morning? Are you crazy? I'm on vacation." With that, she turned and traipsed back into her room. Before she shut the door, I heard her say, "Have a good day and stay out of trouble."

I wondered what kind of trouble she was talking about. Seemed like she got into more trouble than me, with her sexy outfits and her attitude. But, I kept those observations to myself, grabbed the tourist literature off the table, and headed to the bathroom to do a little browsing. That seemed like the most appropriate place to peruse glossy propaganda.

When I emerged ten minutes later, I changed into one of those UV protection shirts I had ordered online before we moved to L.A. I know they don't seem like typical teenage-wear, but I was serious about keeping my skin as pale and freckle-free as possible. One year, when my step-father was still alive and we were on a family vacation in Florida, I fried so badly I was covered in water blisters and got sun poisoning. My face swelled and my lips were a crusty, scabby, painful mess. On the trip back, the flight attendant's pity shone in her eyes and she brought me a cup of ice and gave me a tube of zinc oxide, even though I tried to tell her it might be too late for that. I have learned my lesson. I only go into the sun when necessary, and usually when it's morning or evening. Even though I bought all those t's and tank tops with Ethel, they would be worn under long sleeve, tropical-weight shirts, at least during daylight hours.

I quickly dressed. I placed a sketchpad and some portable watercolors in my bag, along with a bottle of water. Then I ran down the hotel stairs for exercise. I wanted to explore the city of Lahaina a little.

When I returned from touring the town, I found a note on the desk saying Jim and Mom wanted to see me. I banged on the connecting door, not wanting to just walk in and interrupt anything they could possibly be doing. I heard Mom yell, "Come in," so I did. She was stretched out across the bed, looking at a pile of fashion magazines she had picked up somewhere. She was wearing a tropical print dress that I didn't actually remember seeing her try on. I briefly wondered if it was new. The dress was sleeveless and turquoise with vivid orchids or some kind of tropical flowers all over it. Jim was in the shower with the bathroom door mostly open. I averted my eyes from that part of the room.

"You wanted to see me?" I directed my attention to my mother.

"Yes. Have you eaten?" She turned toward me.

"Well, I grabbed some food in town." Certainly she couldn't have demanded my attention just to check up on my nutritional needs. She wasn't usually concerned about my meals.

"Oh. We're headed down to Swan Court here on the property and made reservations for three at nine, if you want to come. But you must dress nicer than that." We both looked down at the jeans I had changed into before I stepped into her room. I was still wearing my sun shirt.

"Ummm…" I wasn't sure I wanted to go with them, but my stomach was feeling somewhat empty.

"Jessica, come on. It's a beautiful place with waterfalls and swans and some Hawaiian dancers—a good way to first experience Hawaii. Now go get dressed."

I guessed I really didn't have a choice. Asking me was just posturing. She was taking this family vacation thing a little too seriously. Just then the water shut off and Jim stepped out of the shower.

She focused her attention on him. "Damn, Jim. Put some clothes on. Jessica can see you."

I cringed, not waiting to catch his response, and rushed through the connecting door. "I'll be ready in five minutes," I said as I shut the door between us.

I shimmied out of my jeans, threw off my shirt, and then

I pulled a simple dress out of the closet. I added sandals and simple silver dangling earrings and a sterling ring. I ran a brush through my stringy hair, debated about putting it up or back or something, but couldn't decide. So, I left it in its straight, natural state, and sighed. I added a little mascara and some lip gloss—never knew if I might meet someone. I took one last look in the mirror, mostly pleased with what I saw.

I knocked on their door, not wanting to catch Jim au naturel again.

He yelled to come in. As I walked through the doorway, he turned toward me. He was zipping up his pants. Just great! I thought, and turned to look at my mother who hadn't moved from the bed and the magazines.

"You look nice, Jess," Jim said. At that my mom turned to look at me.

"Thanks," I mumbled and knew I was blushing.

"Glad you decided to join us," he said, still staring.

"Me too," Mom cut in, looking from me to Jim and back again. I didn't like her look—like bullets should be shooting from her eyes.

"Thanks for inviting me," I said, while I played with my ring and looked toward the floor. There was a weird tension in the room. I sat in a chair and concentrated on the rug.

"Come on, Jim. Finish getting dressed," my mom snapped. I wondered why she was in a pissy mood. I hoped it wasn't because of the paints.

Jim tucked in his shirt and pulled on a belt. Then he actually put loafers on over his bare feet. How retro!

He ran his fingers through his hair and then barked at Mom, "Okay. We're going to be late." And he headed to the door. Mom jumped off the bed and followed closely behind him, silent. I was equally silent and brought up the rear of this unhappy party. What a joy this dinner would turn out to be!

Actually, the restaurant was amazing. It was probably the prettiest place I ever have eaten. Torches were lit around the lagoon where the swans swam, gorgeous waterfalls spilled down lava rocks, a grand staircase provided a majestic entrance to the dining room, and the vaulted ceilings reminded me of a cathedral. The place was extremely romantic and they probably wished they hadn't invited me.

Mom starting tossing back fruity rum drinks almost as soon as we were seated. She ordered me one too, and I was extra surprised when the waiter set it in front of me no questions asked. I sat and sipped it, feeling awkward at their silence and somewhat grown up—in a weird sort of way. Jim drank whisky, straight up—or at least that was how he ordered it. He only had two glasses though and then switched to wine with the dinner.

We started the meal with Dungeness crab cakes, at the waiter's recommendation. But of course, Mom wasn't in the mood to be pleasant, so she ordered what no one else wanted—the sea asparagus. I swear she acted like a pre-schooler with her attitude and pout. She even told us that her appetizer was better than our appetizer. When she said that, Jim ordered her another drink and told the waiter to make it a double. I guess he thought if she was drunk, she'd be happier—or at least civil. Her actions were forcing Jim and me to be friendly, to actually have a conversation, something totally new to us. And I wasn't sure I liked it; I certainly wasn't comfortable with the way things were going.

He asked me about school and if I missed it. Yeah right, like who misses school?

He also asked about my art and if I liked the paints he had had delivered for me. I said, "Thanks." I was polite but tried to keep my answers to as few words as possible. I didn't want to piss Mom off any further. Plus, this wasn't a man I wanted to act all chummy with, as I kept envisioning my painting and how its hands matched his.

As we ate our salads and Mom continued to suck down drinks, Jim wanted to know what projects I was working on. I opened my mouth to tell him about the portrait of Timothy when my mother cut in, "She paints, dammit. That's what she's working on. Even I know that."

Jim turned to her and looked like he wanted to strangle her. Instead he wrapped his arm around her wrist and squeezed. "I know that," he said, staring her in the face. "I was asking about what specific painting she is working on."

"You're hurting my arm," my mother said too loudly, as I slunk down further into my chair, willing this not to turn into a scene. Jim let go, but left a definite impression of his fingers. Mom rubbed her wrist. "Bastard," she mumbled.

Jim ignored her and focused his attention on me. "So, what are you working on?" He glanced at my mother, almost daring her to comment again. She went back to her drink and then signaled the waiter for a refill.

"Well," I said, wiping salad dressing from my mouth. "I completed a portrait of Timothy before we left."

"That's the neighbor kid, right?" Jim asked.

"Uh, yeah," I said.

"I'd like to see it when we get back," Jim said and surprised me.

"Well, we'd have to go to Timothy's. I gave it to him." I said, looking down at my plate.

"That was nice of you," Jim said, finishing the last of his lettuce. "What else have you been doing?"

I was tripping. This was too much. Mom was purposely ignoring us now. She had her back to Jim and was staring out the window. I think he was only asking me questions to piss her off and I didn't know a way out of this situation without pissing him off. I kept being as polite as possible and prayed that dinner would end soon.

The waiter arrived with our entrees, which brought Mom a little more back to the table. She had finished another drink and poured herself a glass of wine from the bottle Jim had ordered.

"So, Jess is going to that Halea-whatever National Park tomorrow, at the crack of dawn, to see the friggin' sun rise." She slurred her words and held her wine glass aloft. "To friggin' sunrises," she toasted.

"To sunrises," we seconded, embarrassingly, and clinked our glasses into hers. She swallowed all the wine in her glass in one loud gulp.

"I didn't know you were going there," Jim said. "I've always wanted to go there, but never seem to have the time when I'm here. How 'bout if I come with you?"

WHAT? "Uhh…" I was speechless.

Mom cut in. "Yeah, sure, go with her, you piece of shit. Send her paints, take her to the goddamn park, go ahead, leave me sitting here in the hotel. Maybe I'll find a cabana boy who'll be more attentive." She was getting loud again. Our waiter looked over at us and so did a few diners sitting near us. I sunk even lower into the chair, wishing I could crawl under the table unnoticed. Instead, I stared out toward the swans, ignoring everyone. I wished she'd just pass out already.

"Karen, you're drunk," Jim said, almost in a whisper, but a stern one. "Just shut up and eat your dinner."

She saluted him; she actually had the balls to salute him, and said, "Ay, ay, captain." And with that, she passed out face first into her plate of food.

Jim quickly motioned to the waiter while discreetly pulling my mother off of the table. I leaned over and wiped her face with my napkin. Mashed potatoes clung to her hair and clumped to her eyelashes. It would have been comical if it wasn't happening to us.

Jim spoke to the waiter and to the manager who had come to our table too. "Could you please get a bellman and have her escorted to our room? I guess all the hours traveling, the time change, and the sunbathing got to her." He shrugged, looked helpless, and slipped the guys a twenty each.

"Right away, sir. Thank you," the waiter said.

They actually brought a wheelchair in for Mom and wheeled her away. Her eyes fluttered briefly and then shut again. God was I embarrassed!

I moved my face closer to my food. Jim picked up the conversation right where he had left off, as if nothing had happened. "So, what'd you say?"

I looked up at him, thoroughly puzzled. "Well, I was going to take the van thing, where they drive you there and then you bike back down. In fact, I already reserved my spot."

"That's okay. We can have the concierge cancel it. It'll be quicker if I drive you. Plus, it'll be fun. We can get to know each another better."

That was certainly what I didn't want—to know him any better. As far as I was concerned, he had saved Mom in some way, since she had no, what my school counselor called, "marketable skills". And for that I was grateful. But I was doing fine by myself painting, babysitting, going to school and the museum. I didn't really need him. And at this point, I wasn't too sure I needed my mother either, not after her horrid display tonight. And I'm sure they didn't really need me most of the time either.

This restaurant definitely didn't need any of us, they'd never allow us in here again. I almost said as much aloud, but caught myself.

"Well…"

"Jess, we'll make it fun. I'm sure you need some fun after the last two hours." He patted my hand and I jerked it away. I didn't see a way out of this.

"Uh, okay. We can go together. But I'm warning you: I'm not sure how long I'll be up there on that volcano. I want to paint what I see."

"Even better. That will give me time to see you work." He smiled, but I couldn't tell if it was genuine. Mom wasn't going to like this one bit.

He must have read my mind because he said, "And don't worry about your mother. She won't remember any of this tomorrow. And besides, I booked her a whole day at Spa Moana as a surprise. She'll be so involved in facials, wraps, and massages that she'll forget about us."

8

There was a slight tap on the connecting door at 3 o'clock the next morning. I said, "I'll meet you in the hallway."

I had dressed in layers, as I had read that the top of the volcano could be close to freezing. I wore jeans and a tank top under a long sleeve shirt under a fleece pullover. I hoped I wouldn't roast on the drive up there. My bag housed a camera, my floppy hat, sunscreen, and my watercolors, paper canvases, and brushes. I had added a bottle of water and a Luna Bar. What a breakfast!

As I opened my door and walked into the hallway, Jim approached me and gave me a hug, kissing the top of my head. My body went rigid. "Good morning," he said. "You look wide awake."

I stepped back away from him. "I am," I said, surprised at how good I felt on only a few hours of sleep. I led the way down the hall to the steps. "This will help get your blood pumping," I said and raced down the stairs.

He kept up easily, his zoom-lensed camera thumping against his chest with each step. He was dressed in khaki convertible pants, hiking boots, and a flannel shirt over a t-shirt. He carried a navy blue fleece pullover. His Oakleys rested on the top of his head, and I noticed he had a baseball cap jammed into his pants' pocket.

"Your mother was sound asleep and snoring," he said as we reached the lobby. "I left her a note about the spa and left word for a wake-up call at nine for her. Just in case she oversleeps and misses her appointment."

"That was nice," I said, somewhat distractedly as I walked out from the air conditioning into the 70-something degree air. I automatically started stripping my fleece layer as we walked to retrieve the car from the valet.

"It'll get cooler the higher up we go," he said, getting behind the wheel.

I shoved my stuff onto the backseat and noticed a picnic basket. Jim turned to see what I was doing.

"I thought you might get hungry so I had the concierge pack us breakfast, or at least something to tide us over. We'll have a real breakfast on the way back from the park."

"Oh. Thanks," I mumbled. "I brought a food bar and some water," I said.

"Well, that's not enough for a growing girl," he said with a smile.

I got into the front passenger seat in silence and slammed my door. I buckled in and turned on the radio—loud—so we wouldn't have to talk too much. I stared out the window at the shadows of passing terrain. Somewhere out there in the darkness were birds and plant life, rare and endangered, that could only be seen on these islands. I planned to find some to paint. Maybe I'd even see a Nene goose, Hawaii's state bird.

Somewhere back at the hotel, probably still in her room snoring, was my mother, who would be waking up with one helluva hangover and who would probably be in a first-rate pissy mood. Glad I wasn't going to be around to share in her storm cloud.

After about a half an hour of driving, Jim broke the noisy silence by turning down the radio and saying, "You know, Mark Twain called this sunrise 'the sublimest spectacle' of his life."

I stared at him, not knowing him to be a reader. "Really?" I asked, not sure how else to respond.

"Yes," Jim replied and smiled. He could tell I was shocked; I could feel it. "And yes, I do read," he added, reading my mind. "But more than that, I love trivia. I excel at it. I'll kick anyone's ass in Trivial Pursuit."

Now there's a hobby to be proud of, I thought. Aloud I said, "Oh."

"You know this place we're going looks like the surface of the moon, right? U.S. astronauts trained for the first lunar missions inside the volcano." He grinned, probably thinking he had wowed me with his knowledge. Actually, all he had proven was that he read the same damn travel guides that I had.

"Yes, and we are traveling from sea level to 10,023 feet in just 38 miles," I added.

His jaw dropped. "So, you researched this, did you?"

"Of course," I said. What did he think: I was a stupid teenager? "And I also know that the volcano hasn't spewed lava since 1790 and that Highway 378, otherwise known as Haleakala Crater Road, contains 33 switchbacks. One of the reasons we had to leave so damned early." I grinned.

"Do you know what Haleakala means?"

"Of course. 'House of the Sun'."

"Do you know the story?" I couldn't believe he was trying to stump me.

"Yes. The demi-god Maui's mom complained that the sun sped across the sky so quickly that her tapa cloth couldn't dry. So, the next day, Maui climbed to the top of the volcano and lassoed the sun and brought it to a halt in the sky. The sun begged to be let go and Maui agreed finally, but only on the condition that the sun slow its trip across the sky to give people more sunlight. I'm not stupid."

"Very good," Jim cut in. "I know you're not. But you do realize that the summit does get 16 minutes more sunlight than the coastline below, don't you? So, it may not only be ancient legend."

"Yeah, whatever. Do you think we'll see a silversword?" I was actually enjoying this banter, and that thought scared me a little.

"A what?"

Ahh-haa. I finally stumped him.

"A silversword. You know, that plant that only blooms once during its 50 year lifespan and then dies."

"Oh yeah, that. I forgot what it was called."

Yeah, sure he did.

"I don't know. They're supposed to be very rare. I mean, we may actually see the plant, but I doubt we'll see one in bloom."

I got quiet then, not knowing what else to say. He must have felt the same way because he turned the radio volume up. Only 10 more miles to go, if my calculations were correct.

After we paid the entrance fee to the park, drove up the road to the parking area at the top, and then parked the Jeep,

we walked up the numerous steps to the summit observa-
tion station. The place was already crowded with people,
some wrapped in blankets, some looking stupid, like they
were on a space mission. And the travel books were correct:
the place did look like the moon, with huge craters and
aridity. Or at least, I guessed that is what the moon would
look like from the pictures I'd seen. Never been there, of
course.

When the sun started to rise, I started to paint it. But then
I realized something: it moved faster than I could convert it
to paper. Photos were definitely the way to go, as they cap-
tured an instance and recorded it forever, to be painted later.
So, I snapped and pointed and zoomed and snapped some
more. I went through several rolls of film, but didn't care. I
was in my element.

Jim's shutter was clicking along side mine. We were
speechless, just taking in all of the brilliant colors, watching
the luminescent orb fill the sky. I was awestruck. I prayed my
photos would turn out, though I was afraid they wouldn't do
the scene justice. I wanted to be able to convey the majesty,
the glory of this sunrise to Ethel and Timothy. And I was
thankful I could experience this vision of nature. I quietly
thanked god Maui, real or not.

After the sun positioned itself in the sky, Jim suggested we
take a short hike in the crater before the long ride back. He
wanted to stretch his legs some, he said, and to get a close
up view. I threw all my stuff into my beach bag and followed
him back down to the car and then we drove to the lower
parking lot, closer to the crater. We followed a well-worn
trail around the side of the volcano, near the road. The park
rangers were gathering a group behind us to do the same.

We walked for sixteen minutes in almost complete silence. Occasionally one or the other of us stopped to take a picture of a cool plant or the awesome view. At one point, I spied what I thought was a silversword in full bloom. Jim pulled out a tour book with photos and we compared the photo and description to the plant growing a few feet from the path. Sure enough, we were staring at the once-endangered phenomena.

"We have to stop here," I said, rooting around in my bag for my paints and watercolor paper.

"You do what you need to," Jim replied. "I am going to walk further down the trail. I'll be back in a few minutes." And off he went.

I briefly hoped the park was safe and then quickly got absorbed in my art. I painted exactly what I saw; then on another page, I sketched the silversword in charcoal. I took numerous photos, from various viewpoints on the trail, careful to stay on the trail, to not endanger or trample anything else that was trying to grow in what seemed to me a wasteland. I felt honored to be here, seemingly in the middle of nowhere, and to see this rare and incredible sight. The gods must have been smiling upon me.

Jim returned and suggested we start back up the path. He didn't wait for my answer; he just kept hiking as he passed me. I followed, not really having a choice. I silently wished my newfound plant friend good-bye and hoped its death would not be harsh. When we reached the parking area, Jim pulled out two bottles of juice and handed one to me.

"Come on," he said and hopped into the Jeep. "I have some things I want to show you."

He took the highway down, passing all the bikers of various ages from the bike tour I should have joined. We also zoomed by a male and female pheasant with a brood of young. I wished we could have stopped for a picture of them.

After driving for a while, he turned off the highway. I was shocked.

"Where are we going?" I demanded.

"I said I wanted to show you something."

He must have seen the worried look on my face because he said, "Don't worry, Jess. I'm not looking for a place to dump your body." And then he laughed and ran his hand over his buzz cut.

I didn't think his comment was funny. I scowled at him.

"Come on, lighten up. Haven't we been having fun?" I had to admit that we had.

"Well, this is just more fun. One of the beautiful island spots I ran across the last time I was here."

Interesting place to run across, I thought. The road was barely a road. More like a dirt hiking path that no vehicle should attempt to travel.

Eventually, we came to a grove of trees. Jim stopped the car and got out and beckoned me to follow. What the hell, I thought. I definitely don't want to sit in the Jeep by myself.

There was a visible trail through the trees and I followed Jim on it. After five minutes of hiking, I could hear water. We had arrived at a stream (or was it a river?) and an enormous waterfall. It took my breath away. I was glad I remembered to bring my bag from the Jeep. I pulled out my camera and started snapping pictures. After the sunrise, this was the second most beautiful sight I had ever seen.

"Wow!" I said.

"Yes. Well, now you know why I wanted you to see it." Jim smiled at me.

"Thanks," I said, and silently added, and sorry I didn't trust you.

"Come on," Jim said, and ran closer to the water. As he was running, he peeled off layer after layer of his clothing, until he was naked. He bellyflopped into the water and from where I was standing, I could see that wasn't the only part of him that flopped.

"The water's great." He started splashing around and tried to splash me as I stood on the shore.

"Is it safe?" I asked, not wanting to get naked, but also not wanting to get in the water if some fish was going to bite my ass.

"Of course it's safe," he said. "Would I encourage you to get in if it wasn't?"

I wasn't too sure of the answer to that so I said nothing and started to undress, but I hid behind a tree to do so. There was no way I was going skinny dipping with my mother's boyfriend. I had my bikini shoved into my bag and slipped it on. Now I was ready to face the world, or at least Jim.

"Hey, what's with the bathing suit, hot stuff?" Jim grinned.

I said nothing and tested the water with my foot. It was surprisingly warm so I dove right in. I swam a little underwater. When I emerged, Jim told me not to get too close to the waterfall, that I might get lost in the currents.

We swam for sixteen or twenty minutes, splashing each other in the water and seeing who could find the most glorious colored fishes. What magnificent colors they had— very artistic, like God or Mother Nature or whoever had painted them in primary colors.

Eventually, we climbed out onto the embankment. I had

turned away from him and was reaching into my beach bag, looking for my towel, when Jim pounced on me without warning. "You look so sexy," he said. He leered at me.

My stomach flip-flopped. "Jim, you're hurting me." He had turned me over and was kneeling on my arms, which were pinned, one on each side of my body.

"You know you like it, you little tease. You artistic types are always into kinky things." What the hell was he talking about? I squirmed and tried to free myself. Where was all this coming from?

"Jim, get off!"

"No," he said simply. "You know you want it."

I thought he was going to rape me, but I was wrong. Instead, he kneeled over me, with his knees on my shoulders. His dick was hard and poking straight out, close to my face.

"Suck on it," he demanded.

I turned my head sideways and squirmed, still trying to free myself. He leaned harder into my shoulders.

"I said, 'suck on it'." He grabbed my head and forcefully turned it towards him. I debated biting it, maybe even off. Lorena Bobbitt would have nothing on me.

He pushed my neck upwards so that my lips were smashed against the head of his penis.

"Now open your mouth."

I realized I had no choice. Better to get this over with as quickly as possible and be done with it. I was afraid of what he'd do to me if I didn't.

I opened my mouth.

When it was all over, Jim turned tender and tried to help me dress. That was really fucked up and I told him to stay away from me, to keep his fucking hands off me. He didn't seem offended, just sad. He kept his distance and then had me lead the way back down the path.

I said nothing the whole time, nor on the whole way back to the Hyatt. I did eat the Luna bar, though, not because I was hungry, but more to get rid of the awful taste in my mouth. I wanted to cry, but I wouldn't give him the satisfaction. I was more pissed off than I had ever been in my life.

When we pulled up to the valet parking at the hotel, Jim said, "Of course, your mother needs to know nothing about our trip except that we both had a good time." He smiled.

Yeah, I thought. Same as always. A good time was had by all.

I wanted to kill him.

Mom returned shortly after we did. I was in my room taking a shower, trying to wash the whole experience away from me. I also brushed my teeth at least five times. I wished I had some Listerine.

Right after I returned to the hotel, I had painted a small picture of Jim sucking on his own dick. Of course I had to make it a lot longer than the puny thing really was for it to be possible—but I can take liberties in my art. After painting the piece, I let it dry while I showered. And then, after drying my hair, I burnt the painting of Jim to a crisp in the bathroom sink. I said some words over it such as, "I hope you rot in hell, you bastard." That was the only way I could think of to exorcise my living nightmare.

The thought of telling Mom had fleetingly passed through my mind, but I knew she'd think I had encouraged it, or at least that's what Jim would tell her. Plus, I wasn't exactly sure how violent he could be. My suspicions were that he could probably be pretty violent. After all, he was

Special Forces, and they pick guys with strange and dangerous abilities for that.

Mom banged on my door as I came out of the shower and announced that she felt great and that we had work to do.

We were on vacation, what kind of work did we have to do?

But of course, I forgot the reason for the trip: to find Jim rental properties to buy. She said we were going as a family to do this. I wanted to look her square in the face and say, "Well, if we are a family, then we are fucked up. We put more than the 'dys' in functional." But, I said nothing like that. I did protest that I was tired and wanted to stay back at the hotel and take a nap and then paint.

She laughed. "That's what you get for getting up so early. Come on, Jess. Jim needs our input."

Yeah, that's apparently not all he needs, I wanted to yell.

She smoothed my hair with her hand. "Ah, Jess, come on. It'll be fun, I promise." Mom looked radiant and very happy. I guess the spa did her good. And I didn't want to be the one to spoil it for her. I agreed to go, but I knew it would just enlarge the hole that was inside of me, having to spend all those hours with the two of them. Especially with him.

So, within thirty minutes of returning to the hotel, we left again, with Mom rambling the whole way there about how wonderful life on Maui was. I didn't know what the hell she was talking about since she had pretty much only seen the airport, the hotel and its amenities, the beach, and some restaurants.

But, checking out the condos was a hoot. I mean, getting

to and from the condos, squished in the Jeep with Mom and Jim wasn't much fun, and was actually kind of tense. I did not want to be in an enclosed space with either of them—too close for comfort. But, visiting the condos and seeing how other people lived was fascinating. We followed a real estate agent, originally from California, whose name was Barbie, around from place to place. Most of the places were decorated in what I have dubbed "timeless tourist"—and cheap tourist at that. By this I mean industrial grade beige carpeting, poorly constructed white wicker couches and chairs with muted floral-patterned, foam cushions, clear glass lamp bases filled with seashells (How original at the beach!) and topped by beige lamp shades, tropical fish shower curtains, glass and wicker coffee and end tables, and cheap-ass, scratchy bedspreads in horrid color combinations that would only be found in cheesy motels in washed-up, rundown, derelict-taken-over shore communities. You know the kind of places, where you can rent a room by the hour or the month.

Anyway, the decor did not impress me. Not even in the expensive places that were more than half a mill. I mean, most of those places had outstanding, first-rate fixtures, kick-ass appliances, incredible ocean views, etc., but they all seemed like they were trying too hard to be expensive. They had no warmth, no style. Just a bunch of stainless steel and granite drawing attention to itself, but no real individuality. As we toured each place, and we saw over a dozen, I envisioned what I'd do with each.

A villa on the beach and next to a golf course was grand, and the best part of all was there would be no one beneath or above you. Barbie declared the place "splendid," saying it was her absolute favorite on the market at the moment. The

villa contained the most expensive fixtures—lights, windows, bathroom and kitchen hardware—but was decorated
in modern golf du jour. The furniture was large and wood-
en, for the most part, with sleek lines and a walnut stain. But
the upholstery on the couch, love seat, and chair was an
antique golf tapestry—the kind where men in white shirts,
vests, those short pants that button or tie directly below the
knee, and jaunty little snap brim hats were posing with their
clubs in front of the ball—very Ralph Lauren masculine
study. The bathroom spigot handles were golf balls, one with
a gold painted "C" for cold, its mate with a gold painted
"H." The coat rack in the entryway was made out of golf
clubs, upended. Even the kid's room had a bed whose mat-
tress sat inside a golf cart. I am sure all that stuff was
incredibly costly, but I mean, too much of a theme can be just
too much. And that place certainly was.

Jim liked the floor plan of the villa and so did Mom. It
was one of the most spacious places we toured, with almost
1,400 square feet of living space, three bedrooms, and two
baths.

The villa would have been so much better with less para-
phernalia and more class. I would remove the golf-patterned
wallpaper from the master bathroom and replace it with
some paint, in a moss green with white trim or perhaps terra
cotta. I'd paint the child's room in a cross between bright
yellow and yellow-gold to reflect the sun and the sand. I'd
even paint a sky on the ceiling, very blue with puffy clouds.
And I'd replace the carpet with something sturdier, either
tile or Parquet or linoleum or something, so you could
come straight from the beach or the course and not worry
about getting sand or dirt ground into the flooring. That
went for the furniture too: something wipe-able, that you

could sit on if you were dirty and it wouldn't be so big a deal. Maybe leather or trendy hard plastic or Plexi-glass or something. There were some designers in L.A. who do amazing things with furniture. Anyway, those were just my thoughts. I said some of it to Mom and Jim and they agreed. I hoped they'd choose the villa. Decorating would be fun.

The last place we looked at was hideous. I don't know who was living there, or if it was a rental property, but it was downright depressing. The walls were painted a shitty brown color, and I mean shit as in that was literally the color. The furniture was steel with white silk fabric, or at least it had been before it had gotten so dirty. Now it was mostly gray and spotty. It was a top floor unit and apparently the roof had leaked because one of the living room walls and part of the ceiling sported water damage and how it had been fixed, or if it had been fixed, was questionable. Jim pushed on the space with his thumb and the ceiling actually moved. Scared the shit out of me! I thought the whole ceiling would fall down on top of us. Because of that, I can't even tell you what the rest of the hellhole looked like. I hightailed it out of there and waited for them on the cement entryway, out from under the roof overhang.

Jim and Mom quickly followed me and I heard Jim say to the real estate agent, "I can't believe they are asking $750,000 for that."

She quickly conceded.

We said our good-byes to Barbie, and Jim said he'd be in touch later about a couple of the properties and he'd maybe want to look at a few more. Then, we took off for dinner to Roy's Kahana Bar and Grill. Thankfully, Mom was in a happy mood. She didn't say a whole lot, but she seemed happy. I guess the thought of buying a vacation home had cheered her, or maybe it was the time spent at the spa. Whatever it was, I was just glad she wasn't yelling, that they weren't fighting, and that we could enjoy a meal together in peace.

Mom and Jim both drank Mai Tais and I had iced tea. Mom wanted to know all about our trip to the national park. Jim told her we had a great time and that now the two of us were the best of friends. Yeah, more like fuck buddies, I wanted to say. My eyes shot darts at him, but I forced a smile and nodded my head. I said she missed such a wonderful experience and should come with us next time. Maybe then you could protect me, I silently added, like a parent is supposed to.

But Mom was off on another topic already, telling us all about her fabulous morning at the spa and how it had done her a world of good. She also oozed about how good Jim was, how special to know exactly what she needed, and how he took such good care of her. I wanted to throw up.

The food arrived and she was quieter, busy eating and drinking more Mai Tais. We all were enjoying our dim sum and imu-baked pizzas. The food was delicious and I loved every scrumptious bite. I was glad Jim had suggested this place. I ate so much; I had no room for dessert and neither did they. We were full and they seemed happy.

But the serenity didn't last long. While we were driving home from dinner, Jim said to remind him to call Barbie, that he thought he'd buy two of the properties we'd looked at. That's when Mom picked a fight with Jim, telling him she knew he was interested in Barbie, that he probably wanted to fuck her. Or that maybe he already had on his last trip to the island. He got defensive, and who could blame him, with her accusations coming out of left field.

Jim bypassed the valet parking this time. I think he knew there would be a scene. When we pulled into the hotel self-parking lot, Mom jumped out of the Jeep and slammed the door, forgetting to let me out. She ran around the car and took a swing at Jim as he stepped out of the vehicle. He grabbed her arm and squeezed. She yelped and cringed. I knew he was hurting her.

I leapt out of the back of the Jeep as she yelled, "Fucker!" and spat in his face.

He took a swing at her with his free fist, hitting her upside the head.

"DON'T hit my mom," I yelled. I flailed out at him with my fists. I had never been so angry. At that moment, more than any other, I truly hated him with everything in me.

Mom was reeling from the punch. I was sure she was seeing stars, as he had let her go and she wobbled, trying to keep her balance, trying not to fall on the asphalt.

Jim had hold of me now, squeezing my wrist, but surprisingly not very hard. "This is between your mother and me," he said, right in my face. "Stay out of it or you'll get hurt. And we don't want that to happen." I could tell he'd make me pay later, but I didn't care.

"Well, you've hurt her!" I shouted in his face.

"Jess, don't." Mom said from behind me. "He's right. I was out of line."

I couldn't believe it. *She* was the victim. Granted, she had started the fight, but he didn't have to hit her, especially so hard.

Jim dropped my wrist and I spun around to look at her. I knew he wouldn't hit me from behind.

Their moment of fury had passed.

"Are you okay?" The point of impact on her head was starting to swell and to bruise.

"I'm fine. Don't worry about me."

How could I not?

"Jim hit me in self-defense. He didn't mean it; he didn't mean to hurt me."

Yeah, right. Like I believed that one. I knew what I saw.

Jim went to her and wrapped his arms around her and hugged her. "I'm sorry," he said. "But you were being ridiculous."

Mom started to cry. "I know, honey. I just get so crazy sometimes. I don't want you to even look at another woman."

"You know I love you, baby." And he gave her a kiss, a passionate one. Right there in the parking lot, in front of me.

I thought I would be sick.

I turned away.

When I glanced back toward them, I saw that they were already on their way through the archway and down the path, walking inside the hotel. I followed in silence, trying to process what had happened. It didn't make sense.

We were all quiet on the elevator ride. Jim had his arms draped around Mom and she stared at the floor. I faced forward, happy that the elevators weren't programmed to stop on every floor, and that we were heading straight up. I didn't want to look at them, nor did I want anyone else to see them. When we reached our floor, they went straight to their room, without a word to me. I just stood and stared, not knowing what to do, how to handle the situation. The only thing I knew for sure was, provoked or not, Jim had hurt my mom. And that wasn't okay with me.

The next morning, while I was in the hazy place between sleep and wakefulness, I had a vision. I saw a dove stumbling unsteadily down a stretch of beach. She had a broken wing that lay limp and was twisted at an odd angle. Her white feathers were covered in pale, but colorful bruises, and her coo was pitiful—soft and almost a moan. Yet, she seemed determined to get wherever it was she was trying to go. Her face wore a look—actually I saw it in her eyes—that nothing would stop her from reaching her goal, even if it killed her trying to get there.

My eyes snapped open and I shook my head, but couldn't shake the vision. My stomach felt like a hollow lump, and a headache buzzed my brain slightly. I had to paint.

I grabbed the watercolors, paper, and brushes nearby my bed and quickly recreated the scene. I figured even if the dove didn't make it, she deserved to be immortalized and remembered. With each stroke of the brush, I became concerned for this envisioned bird and wondered what had caused all her damage. I even ran to my lanai and looked out, making sure there really wasn't a dove staggering uneasily down the stretch of beach I could see from my sliding glass door. And of course, there wasn't. It just all seemed so real.

When I finished painting, I took a shower and dressed for the day. We had no plans that I knew of and Jim and my mom were still locked away in their room, which was good since I wasn't sure if I was ready to face them. I still felt raw from last night.

When they did emerge from behind the connecting door, they appeared happy and all kissy. My mother sported a bump and bruise at her left temple, near her hairline. Mom's glorious, thick hair covered the rest of the remnants of Jim's anger.

"Did you sleep well, honey?" Mom looked at me, but I wasn't sure she was talking to me. She so seldom called me "honey". So I didn't say anything.

"Jess, I'm talking to you. How did you sleep?"

"Oh, sorry. Fine, and you?"

What formality!

"Oh, wonderful. Jim knows what to do to make me sleep like a baby." She squeezed his arm affectionately. I wanted to yell, "yeah, like punch you in the head. That was a concussion, not sleep!" But, of course I said nothing so she continued.

"We had the best sex last night." She beamed and Jim beamed back and caressed her head.

"Mom! Way too much info." I overdramatically covered my ears with my hands.

"Oh, Jess. But I am just so happy. I want to share my joy with everyone."

"But, Mom, really. There're certain things I don't need or want to know." Now I felt like the parent again.

Jim cut in then. "Who's hungry for breakfast? I'll take everyone out."

The thought of eating with the two of them again did nothing for my appetite. "I'll just have cereal here," I said. I had seen pints of milk and small boxes of cereal in a shop downstairs. "I want to get an early start on painting on the beach, before it gets too hot."

"But Jess, we thought we'd all drive the Road to Hana today, that's why we're up so early. It is supposed to be spectacular."

I remembered the travel guide saying the road has the most beautiful scenery on the island, that the journey was the destination. I was tempted and bet I could get some really good pictures out of it—ones I could recreate on canvas later.

"Ummm." I stalled, still not totally convinced going with the two of them was a good idea.

"Come on, Jess," Jim said. "It will be a blast. We can stop and park along the way and bathe under waterfalls."

Damn, he had to bring that up, to evoke those memories. I almost shouted, "Yeah, well, my last experience with you and waterfalls, buddy, was not too positive", but again I just ate the words and stayed silent.

"Please." Mom was pleading now and I couldn't stand it. I caved and raced back to my room to put my swimsuit on under my clothes and to pack up all my supplies for the day-long excursion.

Besides, she might need my protection again.

When I returned to their room, Jim was on the phone. I presumed he was talking to Barbie's machine because he said, "Hey, this is Jim. Just calling to let you know I want the villa and that condo at…" He named some address I didn't catch clearly, nor did I remember. He told her to draw up the paperwork and then he'd see her tonight to sign it, that he'd be out and unavailable most of the day. I guessed this trip had really paid off for him.

When he returned the receiver to the cradle, he turned and looked at me and with a smile said, "I'm happy you're going with us, Jess. It means a lot to your mother and me." I didn't like the way he was staring at me; it sent a chill down my spine.

"Yeah, well, I'm doing it for *her*." I wanted to make that clear.

"Good," he said and rubbed my left shoulder as he passed me to walk down the hall. His touch sent an electric current into me, and not the good kind. The image of an eel came to mind; that's what he was: a slimy, electric, untrustworthy eel.

Before we got on the Hana Highway, we stopped at a gas station to fill up and then stopped in the small town of Paia for breakfast, at a place where you could get omelets and stuff and eat while they made picnic baskets for your trip. The place was called Picnics and had good food, but I thought their name could have been a little more original.

Mom and I got smoothies to go and with that we set out on the incredible Hana Highway. Jim put the top down on the Jeep so we got full views of the scenery. The road was twisty with lots of one-lane bridges. I had never seen so many waterfalls before. There were big ones and smaller ones, single ones and double ones. The powerful force of the water seemed to wash away my negative memories. I was thankful and felt blessed for the first time in a long while.

We stopped frequently to take short hikes and to snap pictures. I remembered the monotone announcer guy on channel 7, what I had dubbed "tourist TV," which was all about Maui and the things to do on the island, say that driving to Hana would take two hours with no stops and around three with stops. The way we were moving, and with all the traffic and with all the stops, we'd be lucky to get there in five hours or more. But I wasn't complaining. This was the first amount of peace I had felt in months, maybe years. We actually seemed like a happy family. Mom and Jim were affectionate, but not overly so. And Jim quit leering at me; if I didn't know better, I'd think from the looks of him that he was a decent human being.

And I had to admit he did have his good points, like buying me the paints and taking us on this trip. During the drive to Hana, he seemed back to the old Jim, not yesterday's Jim. It was like he was schizophrenic: nice Jim/nasty Jim.

Today's Jim stopped the car whenever Mom and me wanted to take a picture or needed a break from the car. We took some crazy pictures. On one hike at a little state park, we found a leaf bigger than my face. Mom had me hold it in front of my face and she took a picture, laughing. She said I reminded her of a Scooby-Doo villain, like a relative of the pumpkin-headed villain.

Jim stopped the car near a cluster of rainbow bark trees and told us to get out, that he wanted pictures of his two girls amidst the unusual trees. Mom and I posed and hammed it up for him and he snapped away.

God, that was what it felt like a long time ago, before we

moved to L.A., before my stepfather killed himself. I remembered when me and Mom used to have fun, when we used to laugh. And when the man in our lives had fun with the both of us, innocent fun, that is. It seemed like another lifetime.

A little closer to Hana we stopped at a volcanic black sand beach at Wai'anapanapa, which is where we ate our lunches. The mosquitoes were pretty heavy on the hike down to the beach. Mom and I sprayed ourselves over and over with bug spray, but it seemed to do no good. I swear, if there's a mosquito within five miles of me, the little sucker will find me. And it wouldn't be so bad if I just got bit and that was it, but the bit area swells all up and turns red and doesn't diminish for days. And the itching is enough to drive anyone crazy.

Anyway, we ate our lunches and Jim splashed around a little in the water. Mom and I stayed on land, watching him. One thing about Mom, she may love the beach, but she isn't much of a water lover. She said when she was a little girl she got caught in an undertow and thought she'd be lost at sea. Because of that, I'd never seen her do anything but walk along the incoming tide. That was as wet as she'd let the ocean get her—just her feet.

The coolest part of our trip was the Blue Pool. We drove down this dirt road that seemed to go nowhere and it just kept going. A few times it even crossed creeks and we had to drive through the water. I was glad we had the Jeep. Other cars, convertible Mustangs and Sebrings, were stopped and stuck where it was muddy or the water was too high to cross. Jim swore the guidebook said there would be a great blue pool and waterfall. And he was right, it just took us a while to find it.

So, the dirt road ended and other Jeeps were parked haphazardly around the barrier at the end of the road, right before a pebble beach and the ocean. We hiked out onto the beach and looked around and couldn't find a pool or a waterfall or even any other people. Jim said he'd go back to the Jeep for the guidebook. I walked further towards the end of the little peninsula of water. Mom followed me, and almost ran into me when I stopped short. "Jim," I yelled. "Found it." I could see the top of a waterfall across the way, meaning we'd have to cross the crashing waves flooding the rocky inlet.

I held my bag high above my head, praying I would find footing that wouldn't put me too deep in the water and that a big wave wouldn't knock me down. Mom actually followed me, breaking her rule of not getting into the water. Thank God we both had on quick-dry shorts and swimsuits underneath, as the water was up to our waists.

"Be careful, Jessica," Mom said. I glanced over my shoulder at her. She looked worried, but I didn't think it was for me.

"Just follow me and stay close," I said to her.

When we reached the other side, I helped her onto the embankment, which was a fairly big step up out of the water. Jim was still crossing, about halfway to us.

"What an adventure," Mom said, scrunching up the bottom of her shorts, trying to get some of the water out. We waited for Jim before we set out across more pebbles toward the waterfall, which could now be seen more clearly. Lots of people wearing swimwear were sitting on the large boulders around the pool. Almost all of them had cameras either around their necks or in their hands. One guy even had a small lounge chair on top of the rock. He had a video camera in his hands and was filming some children who were happily splashing in the pool. The waterfall flooding into the pool was enormous. It started from way high up in the trees above and was probably three stories tall. The water was almost clear to the bottom of the pool upon close inspection; from a distance, it did indeed look blue.

Jim said, as we approached, "The pool is fresh water."

"Oh," I said, not sure it mattered, but it must have to Mom because she stripped out of her wet shorts and climbed right into the water, remarking how warm it was. A few people gawked at her swimsuit, or lack thereof, and at first I was embarrassed, but then I figured, screw them, they're just jealous and they don't know us anyway.

I sat on a warm, dry rock, took pictures of the falls, and then slipped out my pen, paper, and watercolors. I sketched the scene in front of me, complete with Mom and Jim in the picture, and then filled in the colors. A couple of people passed me and remarked how good it was. I smiled, happy to have my talent recognized. One woman asked me if I could paint her a picture of the waterfall and pool and wanted to know how much it would cost. I was surprised. This was my first commissioned piece. Mom heard the lady and beamed at me and said, "Go ahead, Jessica. We're happy to stay here for as long as we need to."

"Thanks," I said, and went to work right away on the lady's painting, while she looked over my shoulder.

"You're very good," the lady said. She was a little overweight and wore a black one-piece suit. She had a beautiful face with vivid green eyes, nearly flawless skin with rosy and chubby cheeks. I really wanted to paint her portrait so I asked if I could when I finished the piece she was paying me for. She said she'd be honored and even started to blush a little. I gave her that picture free of charge, but I took a photo of it and of her beforehand, so I could keep them in my portfolio.

A couple of other people asked if I could do paintings of the waterfall for them too. Mom assured me that they were having a fine time just relaxing in the pool and to keep going. What an easy way to make money, I thought.

By the time we left, I had made over $100. Not bad for a couple hours work. Jim joked that with all the money I made, I could pay for dinner. I laughed. I had seen our dinner bills; each one so far was over $100. Eating out in Maui was not cheap, at least not at the places Jim picked for dinner.

When we arrived in Hana, I was a tad disappointed. The monotone tourist TV announcer said the place had become somewhat of an artist haven, or at least that is what I thought he said. What I saw before me was a frumpy little town that wasn't much of anything. Now I knew it wouldn't have the kind of scene L.A. does or any of the other big cities, but I just expected it to be more special.

I don't know if Mom and Jim were disappointed or not, but Jim didn't even suggest stopping there; he drove straight on through and said we were headed to the Seven Sacred Pools, which featured, you guessed it, more waterfalls and seven pools, or maybe more depending on how you counted.

Tour books and tourist TV rave about the Seven Sacred Pools, but once again I was disappointed. Either that or I was on pool and waterfall overload. Anyway, the pools are located at the bottom of Haleakala National Park. You have to park your vehicle and then hike through a few fields and eventually you emerge through a grove of trees and down some steps to the pools where there's a zillion people in and around the pools, under the waterfalls, taking pictures. It was crazy and way too many people for my taste.

Jim took one look at everyone wandering around the water and said, "Do you really want to do this?" I could tell he didn't.

"Let me just take a picture," Mom said. "And then we can get the hell out of here. I've seen enough natural beauty for one day."

I agreed, not about seeing enough nature, but with wanting to leave.

When we returned to the Jeep, Jim said he didn't want to go back the way we came, but wanted to drive around the rest of the island, around the southern and westward part, back up to Ka'anapali Beach. Mom said something about it being illegal, taking rental cars there. Jim said that was horse-shit, and off we went. And I'm glad we did. That part of the island was unspoiled by development and there were few cars on the narrow, twisty, semi-paved road. I guess the rest of the island's tourists believed what Mom did, that they weren't allowed to drive there.

We stopped a few times on the trip back from Hana. Once so I could take pictures of some old, magnificent church on top of a cliff overlooking the ocean. I'd paint it when we returned home. And once so we could check out some naturally made volcanic rock arches sticking out into the ocean current.

Toward the end of the drive, we passed the highway that leads to Haleakala, the one we took the day before, and my stomach did a flip-flop. Immediately I told myself to get a grip, to remember the fun we had today, that that was what was important.

All in all, the four to six hour trip to Hana and back, took around twelve hours. But they were twelve, fight-free hours and that was what mattered.

11

The last couple of days on Maui were beach days and shopping days and snorkeling days, though I did very little of the latter and Mom did none of it. The reason I did very little snorkeling was that when I tried it, I couldn't get the whole breathing from a tube thing working. And then when I finally did, and got to see some amazingly colorful fish, a big wave crashed me into a coral reef causing me to cut up my leg. I could feel the blood and knew I needed to get out of the water. I thought a shark might get me, as unlikely as that sounded. Mom was on the beach. We were in Honolua Bay at the time. She watched me stumble out of the water with my flippers on, took one look at my leg, and started running towards me. She yelled for Jim, but I doubted he could hear her. He was pretty far out there, in the blue, blue water, with his face down in it, looking for some eel.

Mom wrapped a towel around my leg and told me we needed to go to the hospital. I told her not to be ridiculous, that I'd be fine.

"Jess, water has bacteria and all kinds of shit. We have to get you cleaned up." She looked greenish. Blood was not her thing. She turned toward the water and yelled for Jim again.

I was embarrassed, as the beach was fairly crowded and people were looking at us. "Shh, Mom. I'm fine." But she paid no attention and was actually running into the water, yelling Jim's name.

I flopped back onto the sand, removed my flippers and snorkeling gear, and waited, having nothing else to do. I did inspect the blood once; it was a really vibrant color of red. I'd have to remember that for future creations.

I replaced the towel, not wanting to freak anyone else out. Plus, there were small children around.

Somehow, Mom got Jim's attention because he was swimming towards her. And my mother was near hysterics now, screaming that I was going to die if they didn't get me to the hospital soon, that I was losing lots of blood. I shook my head in disbelief. Talk about an exaggeration.

And when Jim approached me, I told him just that: that I wasn't going to die. I just had some minor scrapes. That was all, but when I said that and looked down at the towel, I was amazed at the amount of blood that had ended up soaking through. I was a fast bleeder, I thought, and that probably wasn't a good thing.

"We better get you to the doctor, Jess. Just to get that cleaned out, if nothing else. There's a doctor's office back at the hotel." He helped me up while my mother gathered up our stuff.

When he tried to put his arm around me, I told him I could walk just fine and didn't need his assistance. I didn't want him touching me—ever again. We hurried as fast as I could go back to the Jeep. Mom was fretting the whole way,

saying I'd better get a tetanus shot, that someone had probably peed in that ocean. And that the fish definitely had shit
in there.

Where else were they supposed to shit? I wondered. After
all, it's *their* home that we invade.

The doctor's office wasn't so bad. Except for the one
receptionist lady. When I came in and she saw the cuts, she
asked me if I or anyone else had peed on it? I looked at her
like she had four heads.

"What?" I managed as politely as I could.

"Yeah. That's disgusting," Mom added.

"Oh, I know about that," Jim said. "Piss is supposed to kill
bacteria. I learned that in the military." He seemed proud of
himself.

The receptionist beamed at him. "So, did you do it?"

"No way," Mom cut in. "Sounds like it creates more bacteria. And nobody is pissing on my daughter."

At least not literally, I thought.

I was glad when the nurse called my name and I could
get away from that creepy conversation. I got a tetanus
shot, had the wound flushed out and then bandaged, and
was loaded up on a lot of antibiotics, and sent home. No
stitches needed. The doc, a gray haired guy with a rip in
his polyester pants, told us that coral abrasions and lacera-
tions were the most common injuries he treated. The second most common injury was eel bites. He explained that
when eels bite people, they grip on, kind of clamping
down on a person's leg or arm or foot. Made me think
they were the pit bulls of the sea. The doctor explained,
complete with pantomimed hand movements, that when
an eel grabs onto a person, their instinct is to pull the thing
off, but the eels' teeth are slanted, causing strips of skin to

be scraped off. I could visualize the flayed flesh.

Cool.

But I wouldn't want it happening to me. I was thankful I hadn't run into any eels out there. I must have been crazy to be out there in the first place. I can't believe I let Jim talk me into it. Mom was right; the ocean was no place for people. At least for people who weren't in boats—but I wasn't sure those were very safe either.

The doctor told Mom to keep an eye on me, to make sure infection didn't set in. But he thought I'd be fine. He loaded me up with large bandages, which I was sure were worked into the bill somehow, and then sent us on our way, after Jim paid with his credit card; the hotel doc took no insurance plans.

When we were done, Jim told me to pick the restaurant and we'd go out and celebrate my almost clean bill of health. I picked Cascades, a hotel restaurant we'd eaten in earlier in the week. They had a sushi bar and sushi was my favorite, particularly unagi rolls—at least eel is good for something.

We took the elevator upstairs to change into nicer clothes first. I was careful to put on a longer dress. I wanted something that would cover up my bandages. I didn't want to display my stupidity to the world.

Once we were seated, Jim raised his drink to me and said, "To no stitches." I smiled and drank to that with the Mai Tai Mom had ordered for me. We had a pleasant meal, and I quietly fed the little sparrows that came to our table to beg for bread. One male even sat on the table in front of me, eating food from my outstretched fingers. Jim took a picture of us and the bird didn't seem to mind the flash.

The restaurant was open on most sides to the beach and

the sunset. It was particularly colorful that night and I got a lot of good pictures from our table and from the small grassy area a few feet away.

We finished off our sushi and all had dessert and coffee. That restaurant made the most incredible coconut crème brulee and it was actually served in a split open coconut with brown sugar and berries sprinkled around the plate.

The hotel had a one-hour photo shop and I asked Jim if I could drop off some film there on our way back up to the rooms. I figured he'd let me and he'd pay for it, but I wanted to be sure.

After that, I stayed a landlubber with Mom and I spent most of my time painting, either in my room, or on the beach, or near the pool. My cuts seemed to heal nicely, with no redness or infection. For that I was happy.

One day while I was on a hammock on the hotel property reading a book, just relaxing, I watched a small chameleon run up the tree the hammock was on. He was by my feet. I had seen little geckos and things back home, but I had never seen a chameleon before. This one had bluish eyes, the color of the Maui sky, and he was kind of a taupe color, but I figured that was because of the tree he was on. The trunk of the palm was that cross between gray and beige. I took a picture of the chameleon, but I wasn't sure he would show up very well. I wished he was green.

But that got me off the hammock on a hunt for more of them. I figured where there's one chameleon, there should be more, so I slowly strolled up and down the paths around the hotel, searching the lush green foliage for more critters. Eventually, near an ancient Thai Buddha, sitting lotus-style tucked away in a natural alcove near a path, I saw another chameleon, a green one. I had never seen an animal such a vivid green color. It was amazing.

I had a strong urge to reach out and touch it, to see what it felt like. It appeared so delicate, with dainty little feet with fairly long but minute nails, a whitish neck and underbelly, and those beautiful blue eyes. He was one of the best looking and most fascinating animals I had ever seen, and I knew he could change in an instant. Sometimes I wish I could do that—have built-in camouflage that would hide me from Mom and Jim and other people when I didn't want to see them or to be seen by them.

I took a couple of pictures of my little lizard friend and then I sat on the walkway. I knew he could be gone any second, but I really wanted to paint him. (Or maybe it was a female. I wasn't sure how to tell the difference with reptiles.) I pulled out my watercolors, paper, and brushes, since that is what I had with me. I didn't think the washed-out colors would do him justice, but I could always repaint him later in vivid oils. I just wanted something to help ensure a correct memory later. It's not always accurate to paint from a memory.

I was surprised the chameleon stayed still for so long for me. I was certain he'd dash off at any second, but it was almost like we had a connection, that he knew I wouldn't harm him, that I just wanted to immortalize his beauty.

So, when I was finished with my painting, I thanked him, and then left him to enjoy his peaceful state on the green leaf.

The one other thing on the hotel grounds that I spent a lot of time studying was the penguins. I don't know why, but the Hyatt has an enclosed desert-like area where five or six penguins live. Each penguin has its own hut, which reminded me of a boulder-shaped doghouse. The penguins stayed in the huts almost all day, only occasionally peering out of the open archways. I think they spent most of their days sleeping. But, towards evening, they got more active and came out and walked around their enclosure. Their designated area had a pool of water in it that was designed to look like a rocky-bottom pond. Not once did I see a penguin go into this water during my whole week in Maui. The only things I saw in the water were dead, very shiny silver fish. And those were resting on the bottom of the pond. I am sure they were feeder fish, but the penguins obviously didn't find them very appealing either, otherwise they wouldn't have been there, uneaten.

I spent so much time watching the penguins because I had never seen a live penguin before; I'd only seen ones on the National Geographic channel. Also, they fascinated me because I thought that penguins lived in cold, icy places, not hot, humid ones with rocky terrain, like Maui. But the penguins looked healthy enough so they must not have needed the Antarctic climates.

Penguins wear very artistic outfits that remind me of sharp, contrasting black and white photos. And I don't think they were all the same kind, as their skin patterns were slightly different from one another, though all of these penguins stood approximately the same height and looked relatively the same. It's just that some had more detailed patterns.

One early evening I took my small easel down to the penguins' domain and put it on the wall surrounding them. I painted a small watercolor of their man-made habitat and then I added a few of the penguins. I created a few different paintings from various viewpoints around the enclosure. One of the penguins seemed particularly interested in me, and he (or was it a she?) waddled closer to me, and stood watching me, as I watched and painted.

I never realized how personable penguins are. I mean, I had seen them on TV belly flop down the ice slides, and I had seen the baby penguins play together. But, these were adult penguins and some of them cuddled with others. And at times they seemed just as interested in the people around them as the people were in them. They were fascinating.

The thing that struck me the most about them though was their serenity. During those seven days, not once did I observe them fighting or squawking or hitting each other. I thought we could do well to learn from them—especially those living in my household.

But I had to admit, those last few days on Maui were more peaceful for me than the other ones. Jim and Mom fought minimally and when they did, they usually resolved things quickly, and with no physical violence. I didn't have to step in and protect my mom, and Jim seemed to be in good-guy mode, buying us presents and paying for expensive dinners.

The morning before we left, Jim called Barbie and asked if he could return to the places he was buying to take room measurements, so we could start planning the décor. I thought that was a good idea, but wanted to go nowhere alone with him. Good-guy mode or not, I still wasn't all that comfortable around him.

He made plans to meet Barbie at ten o'clock at one of the properties and then said he needed my help. Mom was there too, as I was standing in their room. She was finishing her packing. I was already done, but I hadn't mentioned that to them.

"We can all go," I said. "That way it will be done quicker."

"But Jess, I'm not ready," Mom said. She looked into my face. "You and Jim go and then come back and pick me up. We got an extension on the check out and I plan to use every minute of it. I won't be rushed." She put her fists on her hips for emphasis.

My eyes silently pleaded with Mom's. "Mom…"

"Oh, Jess. It's fine. We'll take care of it and then come back and get her." Jim said as he walked into the bathroom and shut the door. I don't know if he had to go or he sensed an argument and he didn't want to hear it. He didn't wait for my reply.

"But I still need to pack too." It came out as a whine and I didn't mean for it to. I hated myself for sounding upset. I couldn't let Jim know he rattled me.

"I thought you were done." Mom was still standing there staring at me. "Then what the hell have you been doing hanging around us?"

"Well…I wanted to see when I needed to be ready." I knew it sounded lame.

She shook her head. "Jessica." She said my name as three drawn-out syllables.

"I'm sorry. But if the three of us go together and measure, we'll be done quicker and then we can finish packing." I tried to hold my ground, but it felt like a slippery slope.

She sighed an exasperated sound. "The things we do for you."

Yeah, like put me into abusive situations and ignore me, I thought. Those are the main things you do for me. Of course, I only smiled and said, "Thanks." I wanted to reach out and hug her, I was so happy not to have to go anywhere alone with Jim, but I knew that would seem too way out there. Mother-daughter displays of public affection, or even private ones for that matter, were minimal between us.

So, we all went and measured one of the golf places and a nice, smaller condo that was a second floor unit—one I hadn't seen before. Or, I should say Mom, Jim, and Barbie measured. Jim handed me graph paper when we got there and told me to do layouts of both of the places, to draw where the windows and doors were in each room, etc. So, I did the rough sketches that would later help us—Jim and me, that is—determine what should go where and what kinds of things we needed to buy.

And I have to say that the project was actually fun. I looked forward to picking out furniture and colors and textures for these two places. I was used to only creating on canvas—paper, cloth, or skin. This would be the first time rooms would be my canvas. I could create interior designed masterpieces. It would be a big job, but hell, I didn't really have anything to do for the rest of the summer. And it would be something different to add to my portfolio.

And who knew, maybe some celebrity would stay there and like what he or she saw and want me to do their place too. I mean, if you are going to dream, might as well dream big, and aim for the stars. Literally.

12

When we returned from Maui on the red-eye, I wanted my life to get back to normal, or at least my version of normal, as quickly as possible. Mom and Jim were still bickering a little—at the condos, on the plane, in the car on the way home from the airport. I actually wished they'd go back to being all kissy-face and lovey-dovey. At least then I didn't have to worry so much about her safety.

Not too long after we pulled into the driveway, the door-bell rang. Mom yelled for me to get it, that she and Jim were busy.

I opened the front door and stood face to face with Timothy, holding a red rose. He looked kind of bashful, but happy, as he handed it to me and said, "Welcome back."

"Thanks," I said, awkwardly.

And then it got more awkward. He said, "I missed you" and leaned in to kiss me, just as Mom appeared behind me. Timothy jerked away from me, his face turning red.

"Don't mind me," Mom said, then added, "Oh, what a beautiful rose! Is it for Jessica?"

Who the hell else would it be for? Did she think he was bringing her a rose?

"Yes, Mrs. Vandermeyer," Timothy said, still trying to recover his composure. "It's nice to have you all home."

"Tim, we've been over this before. Call me 'Karen'."

Timothy shifted his weight from one foot to the other and stared at the ground. "Uh, okay. Well, I guess I'll see you later."

I didn't know what to say, not with Mom standing there, so I said, "Yeah, see you."

As soon as I shut the door, she said, "Awww, that's sweet. I think he has a crush on you. How cute."

I didn't like her condescending attitude. Plus, I didn't think it was sweet at all. This shouldn't be happening. I pushed past her and went into the kitchen to get a vase.

She followed and kept running her mouth, "So, do you like him? Huh? He's kinda cute."

"Mom! Stop!" I couldn't even look at her.

She poked me in the side and started singing. "Jessica's got a boyfriend. Jessica's got a boyfriend." Then she yelled down the hall, "Hey, Jim, I think the neighbor boy has a crush on our Jess."

I cringed. I wasn't Jim's Jess. "Stop it!" I yelled and raced down the hall to my room, slamming the door. I crashed face down on my bed and buried my face in my pillow. I still had the vase upright, clenched in my fist.

"Aww, Jess, come on." I could hear my mom walking towards my door. "Let me in. Why do you have to be so sensitive?"

"GO AWAY!"

"Jessica, come on. Open up. I want to talk to you. I meant no harm."

"GO AWAY!" And then I started to cry. Geez, not again. Why did that happen? It seemed Timothy triggered my tears and that didn't make any sense.

The door burst open. Mom had a credit card in her hand. "Jessica, we need to talk. I don't like doors slamming."

I sat up. "How the hell'd you get in here? You're invading my privacy." I was tempted to whiz the vase past her head for effect, but didn't, knowing she wouldn't have appreciated it and that I wasn't that dramatic.

She sat next to me and ignored my question. "Why'd that bother you? Don't you like Tim?"

"His name is Timothy and we are *friends*, Mom. That's all." I stared her in the face.

"But why all the drama?" She touched my arm.

I flinched and moved my arm. "Because it's my business and no one else's."

"But I love you and want you to be happy. Tim's a nice guy and he obviously cares about you."

"So what." I didn't want to have this conversation.

"You could do worse for your first boyfriend."

"He's *not* my boyfriend," I reiterated, but to no avail.

"Oh come on. Aren't you even a little curious?" She lost me there. "About what?"

"Sex."

I attempted to erase all emotion from my face, and I leaned over to put the vase on my nightstand. "What?"

"You know, sex." She looked so earnest. "You could be each other's firsts. That wouldn't be a bad thing."

Yeah, but this discussion was. "Just leave me alone. We are so not talking about this."

"If you can't talk to me, your mother, who can you talk to? Sex is a natural thing…between two people who care about each other. He obviously cares about you, and you must care about him otherwise you wouldn't have acted that way."

I just stared as she continued. "The Swedes have the right idea…or at least I think it's the Swedes. Virginity is a burden. When you find someone you care about, you should do it, and I should help make your first time special."

I had no idea where this was going, and though the discussion embarrassed me, I was intrigued. What did the Swedes do? I knew she'd continue if I stayed silent; Mom wasn't much for silence.

"I heard that when it's going to be a Swedish girl's first time, the parents make the room really special, with beautiful sheets and candles and everything and that it is a day for celebration. I think I should do that for you. Better that way than the way I lost my virginity, cramped in the back of a Volkswagen in a dark cemetery with Mark whatshisname. I went to high school with him. Anyway, it shouldn't be like that. It should be special."

Ugh! Just what I wanted: my mother involved in my sex life. And besides, my virginity had been taken from me years ago by some older boy in Wisconsin, during a wild party some high schoolers had. But Mom didn't need to know that.

"Um, I don't think I'm ready." That was all I could think of saying.

"Well, you let me know when you are. And really, I don't think Tim would be a bad choice." She patted my hand. "Are you good then?"

"Sure. And Mom…thanks," I said and willed her out of my room.

She got up and walked to the door. "Oh, and by the way,

all locked doors inside this house can be slipped with plastic." She walked out, shutting the door behind her.

Damn! Now I needed to go to a hardware store and install one of those chain locks. I would've installed a deadbolt if I knew how. The chain thing was easier.

I unpacked my suitcase throwing just about everything into my hamper. I put the brushes back in the drawer, along with the charcoal and drawing pads. I said "hello" to the oil painting still on the easel at the foot of my bed, and then I laid back and stared at the ceiling, letting random thoughts swirl through my head. I figured I should go over to Timothy's and apologize for my and Mom's behavior, and to properly thank him for the rose. Though I still wasn't sure how I felt about it. I should also go to the museum and see if Ethel liked the postcard I sent her, and to see if there are any new exhibits. But I felt kind of tired, so I took a nap first.

Four hours later, I awoke to find myself alone in the house. A note on the kitchen counter urged me to reconsider my position on Tim and sex and told me that they went out to dinner and then might see a movie, and not to wait up. Like I even would.

So, I took a quick shower, changed, applied some lip gloss, and went to the museum. Joe opened the door for me and welcomed me back. He said they'd missed me around there, missed my smiling face.

"It's good to be home, Joe," I said, feeling more like the museum was home than the house I lived in.

I took one trip through the museum, through all of the rooms, seeing if anything had changed. Nothing had, which was comforting. At least one part of my life seemed stable. I hadn't seen Ethel, so I stopped at the front desk and asked.

Millie, one of my other favorite older people, was on desk duty. "Oh, honey, haven't you heard: Ethel's sick. Has been for over a week." Her wrinkled face scrunched and she looked worried.

"Oh. I didn't realize. We just got back from vacation."

"That's right. We have your postcard right here. The one for Ethel, I mean." She pulled it from a stack of rubber-banded mail.

"Millie, do you think you can give me her address and phone number? I mean, I know it's personal and all, but I'd like to call her, send her a card, or maybe go see her if she'll let me." I smiled.

"Well, sweetie, I don't think she'd mind, you being a close friend of hers, but I'll warn you. She's not seeing visitors. We've all tried. I made chicken dumpling soup and home-made bread and she refused even that." Millie's face looked stricken, like her feelings were hurt.

"Do you still have some? Maybe if I can get her to see me, I can take her some." I was hopeful she'd see me, as we were closer than she was to any of the other museum peo-ple. Besides, I wasn't planning on asking; I would just show up on her doorstep and take my chances.

"Oh, would you?" Millie asked, and she copied the infor-mation I needed from a thick, three-ring notebook onto a slip of paper.

"I'll let you know when I'll be seeing her." I thanked her and then left the museum. I figured I'd call later and tell Millie that Ethel had agreed to see me in the morning and that I'd stop by the museum for the comfort food first.

On my way home, I stopped by Timothy's to properly thank him, but we don't need to get into all that.

The next morning, after stopping by the museum for the food, I took the bus to Ethel's part of town. She lived in a posh neighborhood with large, single family homes and swanky condo buildings, the kind with the uniformed doormen. I gave my name to Ethel's doorman and he called to check if I was permitted to go up. She wanted to talk to me so he handed me the phone.

"Hi, Ethel. I brought you some soup. Can I come up?"

"Hi, honey. I really don't want visitors right now."

"But Ethel, the museum staff said you haven't seen anyone for over a week. They're worried. *I'm* worried. Please let me come up, just so I can tell them I saw you and you're all right."

She was silent on the other end. "But I look a mess."

"Well I won't tell them that," I said and chuckled.

"Put Harold back on, dear."

I handed the phone to the doorman. He listened and then said, "As you wish, Ma'am." He replaced the receiver.

"She says you can go up. Number 324. Last door on the left when you get off the elevator."

The elevator was the type with an attendant so I didn't have to do anything but say "hello" and then stand facing front. When we stopped, I said thanks, not knowing the proper protocol in these situations. My mind was on Ethel. Why was she being so secretive? People who are sick still need help, and they especially need food. She couldn't look that bad.

But I was wrong.

I knocked on the door and she opened it right away. I gasped.

"What happened to you?" She was wearing a paint-splattered housecoat and very worn slippers. Her left eye was black and blue and her face was puffy. The corner of her mouth was scabbed and was distinctly yellow and purple. And she was walking stiffly. She reminded me of a cheesy horror film, except this was real life and she was a mess. She hadn't lied.

She gingerly sat in a cushiony, leather recliner and told me to sit in a matching chair near her and to put the bag of food on the coffee table. She took a deep breath.

"Jessica, I've had an accident," she said.

"One hell of an accident," I blurted out, before I realized how disrespectful it sounded. "I'm sorry. What happened?"

She stared at me. At least the one eye did. The other eye I could barely see through the swelling. The white of her eye looked red, like a blood vessel had ruptured.

She sighed. "If I tell you, you have to promise not to tell. No one knows."

"I swear," I said, but I wasn't sure I should mean it. Something definitely wasn't right and I wasn't sure no one should know. It seemed to me someone should, someone beyond me. I didn't know what had happened, but it looked like official help was needed.

And boy, was I correct. What she told me shocked me, saddened me, and infuriated me, all at the same time.

Apparently, a man, a young one, with black, messy hair, she said, had entered her condo through her bedroom sliding glass door one night. The doors led onto a little balcony and though they locked, they had no security bar to keep them from being pried. The man raped her and beat her, and he took her money. When he realized she didn't have much money in the apartment, he beat her some more. She kept quiet because he said he'd kill her if she screamed. She did fight him and showed me the bruises on her wrist where she fought against his restraining muscle. I asked if she called the police.

"No," she said. "I didn't want it to get out."

"What do you mean 'get out'?" I was confused.

"You know, when you file a police report, it becomes public record. Some reporter would dig around and find it, do some research, and write a story on it. I don't want to embarrass my son."

I frowned. "This wouldn't embarrass your son."

"Well everyone knows who he is," she said. "I didn't want to cause unwanted publicity for him."

This didn't make sense. "But what about you? Didn't you see a doctor? Don't you want the guy caught?" My voice involuntarily raised; I was furious. How dare someone do this to an old lady. How dare someone do this to my friend!

"I knew I'd be okay. I'm healing. I washed myself when I was sure he was gone."

"But what about AIDS?"

"Jessica, I am in my 80s." She reached for my hand. "If I get AIDS, it doesn't matter. I am at the end of my life anyway."

"Don't talk like that. Of course it matters. AIDS is a horrible disease."

"But it doesn't matter to me. This way, I cause no one any trouble. I'm alive; I'm healing, and I have friends like you. By the time I see my son again, I will be fine and no one will ever know."

"But that's unacceptable, Ethel. What if he does it again? What if he kills someone next time? Then it will be on your conscious because you could have stopped him, could have gone to the police and had him arrested. Now he's free to do it again." My voice was cracking and I had tears in my eyes. God, what would I have done if he had killed her?

"Jessica, it's over. I'm okay. I know it might not make

sense to you, but you just don't understand. My son, he's a very powerful man. He already has paparazzi following him everywhere. The last thing he needs is something like this, something that forces him into the spotlight. I don't want to cause him any trouble."

She was right: it didn't make sense to me. Any publicity this caused would have been good publicity, could have gotten the guy caught. I shook my head.

She took a long look at me and when she spoke again, it finally made sense. We were finally at the truth. "Jessica. I am an 84-year-old woman who has her independence. The first thing that will happen when I tell my son is he'll move me to one of those dreadful senior citizen homes. He'll think I can't take care of myself. I don't want that. I want to die in my own home at my appointed hour. I don't want to be surrounded by a bunch of old farts who play bridge or canasta all day. I want to be surrounded by my artwork, work at the museum, spend time with my friends—do what I want. I don't want my son or some nurse or anyone else telling me what to do. My husband's dead and this is my time, time for my pleasures, for the things I want to do."

I nodded. I didn't agree with her, and I still thought she should go to the police, but I did understand. She was protecting her independence and freedom, something I fought hard to do, too.

"Can I heat you some soup?" I asked. "Millie made it special for you."

She patted my hand. "I'd love some, dear." She smiled.

I got up and went into the kitchen.

"The pots are in the bottom cabinets, spoons are in the drawer, and the bowls are in the top. Feel free to look around for what you need. I'd help, but I don't think I can get up from the chair." She laughed.

"That's okay. You just relax." I put the pot on the stove, the bread in the oven to heat it, and started to get out the butter, bowls, and utensils. "By the way, when did that happen?"

"Oh, about eight or nine days ago," she said.

Great. That's what I thought: before we left for Maui. If I had known, I would have stayed home and taken care of her.

"How was your trip?" She said from the other room.

"Fine. I got to paint a lot on the beach and Jim bought a couple of condos. And I sold my first commissioned paintings, right by the side of a place called the Blue Pool, a natural pool and a waterfall. It was awesome. The rest of the trip wasn't bad, but I am glad to be home." I figured that was all she needed to know, especially after her own tragedy.

I made two cups of tea while I was in there and then found a decorative, pewter tray on which to carry everything. We ate in the two chairs in the living room, in relative silence. This gave me time to look around the room at her paintings. Most of them were in pale or pastel hues and in fact, some of them appeared to be abstracts made with actual pastels. Almost every one had her signature on it. They were beautiful and complemented each other incredibly.

"Your paintings, are they a series?" I asked between spoonfuls of soup.

"No, just six months of my life." That I understood. Every great artist had his period. Picasso's Blue Period was probably the most famous. Art during those periods tended to maintain consistent threads—subjects, textures, colors. I wondered what caused a pale, pastel period. No emotions were associated with pastel colors, as beautiful as some of them were.

I studied each of the works individually. She used such broad strokes of color and left very little white space. The pieces added dimension to the room, which otherwise was rather bland. All of the sitting pieces were leather—an off-white leather—and the throw rug was an incredibly muted Southwestern abstract in mauves and cornflower blue and seafoam green. The coffee table was cold—glass and shiny, silver metal. All of it looked expensive.

Ethel must have been watching me look around because she said, "My son, dear."

I blinked and didn't get it.

"He had the whole place decorated before I got here. Said he had it designed around my pastels. He remembered those from childhood and said our old, heavy wooden furniture, our antiques, didn't do the pieces justice. He said that I needed a showplace for them. Some gay designer with very good, but very expensive taste, created this place for my art." She smiled weakly.

I couldn't tell if she was proud of the place or felt like a china doll on display, so I said, "Oh, well, it is beautiful."

"Yes, I guess it is," she said and stretched to put her bowl on the coffee table. She winced.

"Here, let me do that. In fact, since we're done, let me do the dishes and then I'll leave so you can take a nap."

"You are a dear," she said as she readjusted herself in the chair and put the footrest up. "Can you get the blanket from the foot of my bed too, before you go?"

"Sure, Ethel. Do you need anything else?" I asked from the kitchen.

"A glass of water would be nice. Just put it on the coffee table here."

When I came back into the room, after washing the

dishes by hand and getting the blanket and glass of water, I found her asleep in the chair. Her head was tilted slightly back and her mouth was open. She reminded me of a baby bird waiting for a worm. I hoped that position wouldn't hurt her neck later.

I moved the phone from the other side of the room to the end table next to her—it was glass and metal too. On a pad next to it, I wrote my name and my phone number, in case she needed me in an emergency. I also wrote that I'd be back tomorrow.

Then, I walked back into the bedroom with a broom I found in a kitchen closet. I shut her bedroom door, stood on the broom handle, and pulled the bristled end up with all my might. It snapped with a loud crack. I took the jagged edge and jammed it into the sliding glass door track and hoped she didn't mind. I didn't want that creep coming back.

I checked on her again and tucked the blanket more firmly around her. I stared at her one more time, feeling anger rise in me. I kissed her forehead and then quietly let myself out.

I went home, once again to an empty house, but locked myself in my room anyway. I got out my pad and pencils and plopped on my bed. I started drawing. Occasionally, I'd close my eyes and feel tears of rage try to escape, but mostly I just kept my head down and drew. Within the hour, I was finished with that part of it. I had drawn Ethel, puffy face and all.

Next, I put the drawing on my easel and got out my watercolor paints and brushes. I ran to the bathroom and filled a plastic cup with water. I added the pale yellow, the purple, the blackness of her bruises. As I painted, a tear occasionally escaped and ran down my face. But I kept going. I had to exorcise this emotional demon. If I had known what her attacker looked like, I probably would have painted him too—and then burned the painting. I didn't believe in voodoo, per se, but I believed that art had power—even destroying art had power. But, since I felt helpless to destroy him, I did the next best thing. When my beaten and battered, painted Ethel was done, I drew a new portrait of her, this time healthy, with a smile on her face and a sparkle in her eyes. To this drawing I added rosy cheeks and a lavender tint to her hair, just like she usually looked. Maybe my good thoughts would speed her healing. I'd take her the positive painting tomorrow, so she could look at it and be comforted with how she used to look, and would soon look again.

13

The next day when I returned to Ethel's, the doorman let me go right up. In fact, he even handed me a key and said that Ethel had requested I let myself in. I was carrying the painting of a healthy Ethel under my arm, and the doorman saw it and asked to see it more closely. "It's beautiful, miss," he said. "A real likeness."

I blushed. "Thank you."

I hugged the painting to my chest as I got onto the elevator. The elevator operator just glanced at it and me. He said he already knew which floor. I just smiled and said, "Thanks."

I knocked lightly on the door with my knuckles to let Ethel know I was out there and coming in. And then I did. She was sitting in the chair where I had left her yesterday, but she had changed her clothes so she must have gotten up at some point.

"Oh, Jessica dear, so good to see you." She extended her hand out to me. "I'd get up, but I am stiff today. Old age is catching up to me." She smiled.

I grasped her hand gently after setting down the painting against the other chair. "How do you feel today, Ethel?

"A little better, but not as good as I once did." She smiled again, weaker this time. "What do we have here?" She looked at the painting, or actually the back of the canvas, as I had the painting part facing the chair.

"A present for you," I said and spun the picture around. "Inspiration to get you better."

"My, she is a handsome one," Ethel said and chuckled at her joke.

I grinned. "Yes, she is and she needs to look like this again, and soon." I handed her the painting. "It's for you."

"Thank you. I don't think anyone's ever painted for me, especially not a painting of me. Can you prop it against the wall across from me so I can look at it?"

"Sure. Would you like anything? Have you eaten?"

"Is there any of that soup left?" She was still staring at the painting.

"I'll check. But I will make or get you anything. What're you in the mood for?"

"Oh anything. I don't have much of an appetite today."

"But, Ethel, you have to eat."

She smiled weakly. "I know, dear, I know."

I went into the kitchen to check on the soup. There was none. Ethel must have finished it for dinner yesterday. Oh well. Her refrigerator and cupboards were fairly bare so I thought pizza or Chinese food might be a good idea. I asked and she said she preferred Chinese, that there was a wonderful little place around the corner who served food with no MSG. Sounded good to me too.

She insisted on paying and sent me off to fetch the food, after calling them on the phone (she had their number memorized) and ordering.

The man behind the counter at the restaurant said, "Miss Ethel say she been sick. You tell her, eat soup. I put special soup in bag. It help her. No charge." He smiled, displaying very straight little teeth.

"Thank you," I said, gripping the bag and accepting the change from Ethel's twenty. I put a couple of bucks into his tip jar on the counter and knew Ethel wouldn't mind, that she'd even expect it.

When I returned to the condo, Ethel was watching a soap opera. I set up a TV tray in front of her and another in front of my chair, and then I dished out the steaming food. It smelled heavenly.

"I don't know why people watch these stupid things," she said. "I have tried to understand it while I have been home. What's the allure?"

I shrugged. I hated soaps, myself, and thought them a waste of time, especially when I could be painting.

"They're so unbelievable. Just filled with beautiful people, more beautiful people than exist in real life, and they have no real life problems. They don't teach a person anything." She shook her head in disgust and shut off the TV using the remote.

She looked down at her tray. "Did Li give me this soup? He's always saying it will help me, help keep me mentally sharp." She expelled a throaty laugh.

I laughed with her, but I wasn't quite sure why.

I hurried into the kitchen to make tea and to get some real silverware. I couldn't stand to eat my food with plastic utensils. And Li forgot to put any chopsticks in the bag, just the cheap-ass bendable plastic forks.

When I returned with two teacups and a ceramic teapot, plus the silverware, I found Ethel happily eating her egg roll. She was trying so hard to be proper and polite and to take small bites, but the swelling on her face and lips and the egg roll's clumped together contents weren't making it easy. I delicately handed her a napkin.

I went back to Ethel's every day for a week total. I didn't see much of Mom or Jim, but that was fine. We had our own lives; thank God.

With each day, Ethel seemed to be improving. Her coloring came back and the bruising faded along with the swelling. Her spirits returned too. We ate lunch (usually food I picked up from somewhere), played card games (I got very good at gin rummy and pinochle), and talked. I felt closer to her than to anyone else in my life. We were almost as close as Mom and me were at one time, during the depressing period after my stepfather killed himself.

I told Ethel about Timothy, not about the sex, of course, but that I was sort of seeing him. She was thrilled for me and said that when she was feeling better, she wanted me to bring him over for dinner. Then she told me all about her first boyfriend and how he took her to the movies and to the soda shop. They also went dancing a lot. Ethel said she broke his heart; he wanted to get married and her father thought she was too young. He wanted her to go to college, which was rare in those days. And she listened to her dad and went to school to be a teacher, an art teacher to be precise. She said she dated a little while she was in school, but no one was as special as her first love. Then, at the first school where she worked, she fell in love with the principal and married him and he was her late husband. She looked a little melancholy when she talked about him. I guessed she missed him terribly.

Ethel asked me if my mom and Jim would be getting married. I told her I didn't know, but I didn't think so. Or at least no one had mentioned it to me. Mom had always said she had bad luck with marriage, so she wasn't sure she wanted to do it again.

"Considering the past circumstances, that's understandable," said Ethel. "You'd just think marriage would provide her with more security, especially since she has you."

I personally didn't believe marriage equaled security, but I kept those thoughts to myself. Aloud I said, "I'm not sure if she thinks Jim is the right one." Mom had never said that, but I certainly felt that way. Of course, Ethel didn't know about Jim's involvement with me, or abuse I should say. I didn't even want to think about it, let alone talk about it to anyone. The more people who knew about it, the more real it would become, or at least that's the way I felt.

Ethel asked if I liked Jim. "Yeah, sure." I automatically replied.

"Really?" she asked, as if for some reason she didn't believe me.

"Well, not always. But no one likes a person all the time, especially a person you have to live with. Besides, what matters is Mom and if she likes him and is happy—and she seems to be most of the time—so it works for me."

Ethel stared at me incredulously. "Sometimes it isn't so easy to get along with a new stepparent, especially after it's been just you and your mom for so long."

I changed the subject to art, our favorite topic. She asked me if I really and truly liked her paintings, the ones in her living room. I said, "Of course. Why?"

"Because, Jessica, if anything happens to me, I want you to have them." She smiled.

"What? Won't your son want them?" I looked from painting to painting and then back to her.

"Oh, honey, he's not interested in my artwork, really. He

prefers popular, modern artists like Andy Warhol—anything that is worth a lot of money. He has an extensive collection that he shows off."

I stared at her, not sure if she sounded a little bitter or amused. "His old mother isn't avant-garde enough." She chuckled.

I didn't know what to say, so I simply said, "Thank you, Ethel. I'd cherish them. But you aren't going anywhere."

"You never know, dear, when it's your time. I wanted to make sure you knew though. I called my attorney yesterday and he's going to make sure it's all taken care of."

I reached across the space between us and patted her hand. Tears formed in my eyes. I knew how much these paintings meant to her. "Thank you."

"Oh, and take the one of me too, the one you did. It's very good." The painting was still where I left it, across the room from her chair, on the floor, propped up against the wall.

At the end of that week, Ethel was feeling well enough to go back to work. I was already at the museum when she arrived, looking lovely in her lavender outfit. Her bruises were gone and all of the swelling had subsided. She thought she was coming in to start her shift, but Millie had actually asked her to come in an hour earlier than that because we had planned a surprise welcome back party. I helped hang the banner. Millie had bought a special cake with one layer vanilla and the other layer chocolate and whipping cream frosting between the layers and on top that was embedded with fresh strawberry pieces. Other workers and volunteers had made coffee and tea; some had brought bottles of wine. The curator had brought three kinds of ice cream. It was quite an occasion.

And Ethel really must have had no idea. When she walked into the employee lounge, there we all were with balloons and music and all of the food. "Surprise!" we yelled. Her eyes widened, filled with tears, and she laughed.

"For me? Oh, I love parties." And she greeted all of her friends as if she hadn't seen them in ages, and I guessed two weeks in self-imposed exile from all friends but me could seem like ages.

She approached me and gave me a hug. "I can't believe you knew about this, dear, and didn't tell me."

I looked her in the face. "Hey, I can keep a secret."

"You certainly can." And she squeezed me gently again.

Everyone was so glad to see Ethel; you could read it in their faces. She was loved by those at the museum, probably by all who knew her. Each person greeted her and hugged her and gently asked how she was feeling. They all said they wished her well. We had all chipped in and bought her a gift too, which was presented to her before we ate the cake and ice cream.

The gift was elegantly wrapped in silver foil paper with the outlines of dark green paisleys. The green ribbon matched perfectly. Ethel opened the box to reveal a lead crystal female artist standing before an easel and canvas, paintbrush in one hand and palette in the other. I had seen a picture of the piece, but never the actual gift. It was gorgeous—and heavy. Ethel picked it up to exam it and then quickly put it down, saying her full strength had still not returned and she didn't want to risk dropping it. Everyone laughed at that. Someone even offered to keep it for her until she felt ready to provide it with an adequate home.

The cake was absolutely delicious, so moist and rich, but not overly so. I wrote down on a scrap piece of paper the name of the bakery, thinking I'd have to remember it for Mom's birthday in September.

The party lasted way past the start of Ethel's shift, but Millie said she'd cover it, and that seeing and spending time with friends was more important. As she left, I cornered Millie and thanked her for inviting me—especially since I was the only non-staff or volunteer person there.

"But you're her family, dear," Millie said and patted my arm.

In some ways, I supposed she was right. I thanked her again and went back to join the rest of the throng, where Ethel resided as queen. She needed this after her trauma and recovery. And I was elated to see her so happy. It was good to have her back at the museum.

14

When Ethel went back to work I finally felt as if my life had returned to normal. I mean, while she was recovering I spent every afternoon at her house, keeping her company, and helping meet her needs. Then, about every other day, I would drop by the museum with a bogus report on how her "flu" was going. Ethel and I had planned out the stories together so if anyone asked, or called her, they heard consistent stories.

Every evening of that week I spent painting, since I didn't get to do too much of it in the afternoon. One night when Jim was away who knew where, Mom came bounding into my room without knocking and said, "I have an idea."

This should be good, I thought. "Yes?"

"I want you to paint me." She grinned and I knew I was in for trouble.

"Do you mean paint a picture of you?" For a moment I was worried she had broken into my private drawer and seen the photos.

"Yes, paint a picture of me." She looked confused, but still happy. "How else would you paint me?"

"Umm, like before. When we did the tattoo."

"Oh, no, not like that. Though I'd still like to get one of those." She sat on my bed. "I want you to paint my picture."

"You mean a portrait?"

"No, me. All of me. Nude."

Oh, no, no way. An artist has her limits and staring at Mom's naked body definitely exceeded mine. "Uh, why?" I knew I'd regret the question the moment it popped out of my mouth.

"It'd be a great Christmas present for Jim."

Where'd she expect him to hang it? His office? The living room? I didn't think so.

"Are you sure that's what he'd want, Mom? I mean, he already has you." I smiled and tried to sound sincere.

"Oh. He'd be thrilled. It's such a good idea. So, will you do it?" She started stripping right then and there.

"WAIT. I can't do it now. I'm busy." I looked at the canvas on my standing easel and implied it was my current project. It was actually a painting I finished a couple of days before but she didn't know that.

"Oh. Well, when then? I want to get started right away. And I haven't had that much time to talk to you about it, what with you spending all your time with your sick friend."

But I've been home every night, I thought. Where have you been?

"We can start tomorrow, if you want. But the thing is, this isn't a short project. You will have to pose—that means be absolutely still—for hours at a time, for days."

"Just how many?" She looked concerned. In many ways, Mom was like a pre-pubescent boy with ADD.

"Oh, at least thirty or forty hours if you want it done in oils." I knew it wouldn't really take me that long, not for the kind of work I did, but I wanted to dissuade her.

"Oils would be the best. All the great nudes are done in oils, right?"

"Yep."

"But that's a long time. Like more than a day." She looked disheartened.

"Yep. Great art takes time. It doesn't happen instantly." I smiled and picked up one of my brushes and a completed canvas for emphasis. "I mean, these took weeks to complete." That was definitely stretching the truth. As you know, most of my masterpieces are imagined and then created in hours, if that.

"It would be a shame though not to immortalize my glorious body." Mom looked down at her chest and legs, which were far from covered in her v-neck tank top and her short shorts.

I cringed.

"When I am old and gray and saggy, God forbid, I want something to remind me of my younger days, proof if you will, that I was once pretty damn sexy. And I want Jim to remember it too." She flashed her bleached teeth at me.

I knew what I had to say, though I hated myself for saying it. "But, Mom, you'll always be sexy. Plus, if your boobs start to sag, you can always get them fixed. You can get it all fixed. How do you think Joan Rivers stays in such good shape? Though she does look like she's had one face lift too many." I grinned what I considered to be an award-winning smile.

"Yeah, I know, surgery is always an option. Nothing wrong with that. All the beautiful people do it. So, will you paint me? Can we start tomorrow?"

I knew I'd never win this one so I told her sure. But we'd have to start in the late afternoon, when the light was still good. And she agreed.

Then I told her I had work to do and needed my privacy. The evening had already started off as too weird. I locked the door behind her as I heard her say she was meeting some friends for drinks, as Jim had a business thing, and for me not to wait up. Like I ever would.

I worked on an abstract pastel sketch as something to do, to pass the time until I heard her leave. I swear her request had sucked the creative juices right out of me. When I thought of it, an involuntary shiver traveled down my spine and I couldn't concentrate. A multi-colored chalky mess was appearing on my paper. It reminded me of a grade schooler's drawing and irritated the hell out of me. I ripped it to shreds.

As soon as her car left the driveway, I unlocked my door and went into the bathroom to wash the pastels from my hands. I started to wash my face and then realized taking a shower and changing clothes was a better decision. So I did, and then I went over to Timothy's.

I hadn't seen him a whole lot since we had been in Maui, and then I spent my afternoons at Ethel's. I mean, we hooked up once the day I got home, but so far, that had been it. So we were extra excited to see each other, and I mean that in a purely sexual way. Let's face it, sex can be a good tension releaser and my life was fairly tense. And for some strange reason, every week it seemed to grow tenser.

Timothy's mom was at work again. When I arrived at his house, he had been playing video games on the computer against some guys in Japan, Australia, and Germany. He proceeded to tell me all about, but I stopped him with a firm and yearning kiss. I didn't mean to be rude, but to me, it sounded like Martian-speak. I didn't understand a word.

I mean, I know how to use computers and I love surfing the Net. What teenager doesn't? But I have no use for video games or cyber worlds or make believe that isn't going to further a vision or enlighten an audience. Even though most video games use a lot of art, I don't consider them Art. They're just some extension of some poor sap's imagination who can't stand to deal with life, with the real world.

Not that I was knocking Timothy for playing them. To each his own, as someone once said. As long as he didn't expect me to play, and he didn't try to explain them to me.

The kiss worked because he shut up, or at least he quit talking. (Shutting up kind of implies that his mouth was closed and it wasn't. It was very much open and his tongue was exploring my mouth and possibly even my tonsils.)

"I've missed you," he gasped.

"Me too," I said, and started to unbutton his shirt.

And well, I won't go into any more details, except to say a lot of tension was relieved that evening.

Timothy and I went out afterwards for ice cream at that place that mooshes the toppings of your choice into the flavor of your choice. The place was surprisingly empty, so we got a table for two, way in the back, away from everyone else. I looked around and saw that the coast was clear and fed Timothy a taste of my ice cream from my spoon. And then I sampled his. It was almost like a real date, but I still didn't want anyone from school seeing us. I guarded my privacy, like the Catholic Church tries to guard a nun's virginity.

Timothy, for once, was fairly talkative but he picked a

very uncomfortable topic for me. He said he had watched some special on TV about teenage girls and abuse. He said a large percentage of females were sexually abused or raped, something like one in four. He wanted to know what I thought about that. I wanted to know why he brought it up, but I was too chicken to ask. I wasn't sure I wanted to know the answer.

"Yeah, probably," I said. "I know some girls, some women even, who have been raped." Just like me, I silently added, but would never share that with him.

"Yeah, but do you think it's really twenty-five percent of the female population? That seems awfully high." He was looking me straight in the eyes and that made me extremely uneasy.

"Well, let me think," I said, stalling for time and giving myself an excuse to look away. I looked to the ceiling and pretended I was counting.

He waited, staring intently, not even eating his ice cream.

"Sounds about right to me. Like I said, at least from the people I know. But I'm not an expert on the subject."

"You think one out of four girls at school have been raped or sexually abused?"

"Probably," I said, taking another bite and licking the spoon. I wished I could change the subject, but I couldn't think of a tactful way to do so.

"But there are thirty-two hundred students at our high school and at least half of them are girls. So that would make 400 of our students who have been raped or sexually molested." He looked incredulous.

I shrugged. "Yeah, probably."

"But doesn't that seem high to you?"

"I don't know. Like I said, I'm not an expert. Does it

matter?" He was freaking me out. Especially the way he was looking at me, so intently, like he wanted to ask me something but was afraid to.

Finally, he looked down at his melting ice cream. "No, I guess not. It just seemed weird."

No, this conversation was weird, I thought.

He looked up at me again. "And the program said that almost half of the rapes go unreported."

What did he expect me to say? "Ummhmm," I murmured. And you're looking at the victim of one.

"Why do you think a girl wouldn't report it? That's just crazy."

No, you are, I started to think. You, Jess, are crazy for sitting here listening to this.

"Maybe the girls are embarrassed or maybe they're afraid." I felt myself getting defensive.

"Well, that's just stupid. Being forced to do something against your will isn't anything to be embarrassed about. If anything, the asshole who did it should be embarrassed." He stared straight into my eyes when he said this. I looked down, wondering how he knew. He seemed to know, and I didn't like that. I didn't want him to think about me that way, as a sorry-ass victim, or to pity me.

He finally finished his ice cream.

I didn't want to look at him.

"Can we go?" I asked, standing.

"Sure. But don't you agree? It's the guy who should be embarrassed?" He opened the door for me and I walked in front of him.

"Uh, yeah. Can we talk about something else? This conversation is a downer." I smiled what I hoped was a charming smile.

"Oh, sure, sorry. So, what do you want to do now?" We were walking back down the street toward our houses. "We could go to the movies."

"Nah. I'm kinda tired," I said and faked a yawn.

"Oh." He definitely sounded disappointed.

"But not *that* tired," I said, as I pinched his ass and hoped nobody saw me.

He grinned and tried to put his arm around me, but I shrugged him off. "Not here, where everyone can see."

"Oh, sure, it's okay for you to pinch me but it isn't okay for me to show you affection." He pouted but I knew, or at least hoped, he was kidding. I knew getting his mind on sex would take his mind off of our depressing ice cream conversation. And I pretty much was willing to do anything to purge that from my mind.

"I'll race you back to your house," I said and took off running down the street.

By the time I left Timothy's house again, it was after midnight. My house was still dark and neither Mom's nor Jim's cars were in the driveway. I let myself in with my key, went to the bathroom to brush my teeth, and then went to my room. Usually, I locked myself in when Jim and Mom were home, to secure my privacy, but for some reason I didn't. Maybe I was too tired from all the sex with Timothy. I don't know, but I did regret it.

Incoming headlights flashed across my window around two o'clock. They woke me, but barely. I figured it was Mom coming home, and in the haze of sleep, I must have ignored it. The front door opened and shut and their bedroom light turned on and their door shut. That was what registered, sort of.

Later, and I'm not sure how much later, my bedroom door opened, but I slept through it. Until the door opener, reeking of alcohol, stumbled toward me and tripped into my bed, landing on me.

"Jess," Jim said as he exhaled lethal fumes at me. His breath had to be 100-proof. "Where's your mom?"

"Out with the girls. Get off me." I tried to wriggle out from under him.

"When's she coming home?" He pinned me.

"Any minute," I said, wishfully.

"Good. This won't take long," he stammered in his drunken state and pushed the covers down to the end of my bed.

"Jim, get off. You're hurting me."

"It'll only hurt a minute." He laughed, sickly.

"NO!"

"Shh." He covered my mouth with his large, hairy hand. And he pushed down my pajama bottoms with his free hand. His body was dead weight on top of mine.

I still tried to wriggle free.

"Stop," he hissed. "You're making this too difficult."

Good, asshole, I thought, and continued to squirm.

"Don't make me have to hit you."

I stopped moving. I knew what kind of damage he could do. I stayed perfectly still and felt his dick try to enter me. It wasn't easy; I was bone dry, completely unaroused. I was surprised he was able to get it up with all the liquor he must have drunk. He poked and poked until he succeeded.

I felt the tears well in my eyes. I shut them tightly, not wanting him to see me cry.

And then the headlights shone in my window and I heard Mom's car door slam.

"Shit," Jim said and rolled off of me and staggered into his own room and slammed the door.

I got up and locked my bedroom door. I crawled back into bed, under the covers, and let the tears fall.

The next morning I practiced my own version of voodoo. I painted an acrylic of Jim's face, a portrait really, as accurate as I could make it. Accuracy was essential, as I wanted to make sure it looked like him and no one else. When it was complete, I stood a few feet from the canvas and took a long gaze at the man I hated. Then I spat and the globule landed right on his eye. I christened the other eye as well the same way. I inhaled deeply. Then picked up my black paint and a very wide brush and painted over his face, erasing it from the canvas and hopefully from my life. When the canvas was completely covered, I felt a sense of relief, but only a minor one. Another thing had to be done to make the process final, but that would have to wait.

I ran into my bathroom to shower and dress. No one in my house was awake, and I didn't expect them to be. The hour was still early. Mom and Jim would probably both have blinding headaches and hangovers, and I had no desire to be around for that.

I dressed quickly and silently. Then I grabbed the painting, which was almost dry. Gotta love that about acrylics: their fast dry time. I also grabbed a Luna Bar, a bottle of water, and some matches.

A park located a few blocks from my house had these great barbeque pits. As much as I hated to destroy any form of artwork, what I was about to do was totally necessary. Fire cleanses.

I put the painting into the grate and piled some dry leaves

on it. The leaves ignited instantly, which in turn torched the canvas. I said a silent prayer that the symbolic would become reality. Not that I necessarily wanted him to burn, other than in hell, but that he'd be gone, gone from our lives, gone from my nightmares.

I watched the fire devour the picture until it was transformed to ash that fluttered and blew in the light wind. And I finally felt a spark of life ignite inside of me, in that place that had been dead for so long.

15

During Ethel's second week back at work, she invited me and Timothy to dinner at her house. All Timothy knew was that she was my friend and that she was old and recently sick. I had also told him about her being an artist and art teacher. I didn't know what else to say, and figured he needed to know nothing else.

We arrived at seven, which was the appointed time. I greeted the doorman and elevator operator by name and Timothy seemed impressed. He had dressed up for the occasion, wearing clean chinos and an oxford shirt. He was also carrying flowers and a box of candy, overkill if you asked me, but I was sure Ethel would find it sweet.

I rapped on the door and awaited her "Coming," but it never came. I knocked again and called, "Ethel, it's us."

Still nothing.

I had my key to her place but felt weird about using it. I told Timothy to bang on the door, while a sick feeling came over my stomach. "Never mind," I said, more harshly than I should have.

I used my key, pushed open the door, and went running into the condo, knowing something wasn't right. I yelled her name repeatedly. She wasn't in the living room or in the kitchen. I checked the hall bathroom on my way to her bedroom. I was afraid that bastard had come back, that she had forgotten and had taken the broken broom handle out of the sliding glass door. But then I found her, lying on her bathroom floor, completely still. Her skin felt cold to my touch.

"Timothy, call 9-1-1. Then call downstairs!" I screamed.

He picked up the phone, and I assumed he was talking. I heard nothing except what sounded like a freight train racing through my head. The noise was almost unbearable. I kept shaking Ethel and calling her name, willing her to open her eyes and talk to me, knowing it was too late, but not knowing what else to do.

Tears flooded my face. Timothy came into Ethel's room and said the medics were on their way and so was the building manager. He left the front door open for them. He reached towards me but I brushed him off, and I cradled Ethel's lifeless body.

"Jess," Timothy said quietly, "Come on, there's nothing you can do."

"SHUT UP!" I yelled, knowing I was being crazy, but I couldn't help it.

"Shh," he said and got down on the floor with me. He encircled me with his arms. "Let it out. It's okay to cry. Just let it out."

"She was like a grandmother to me. She was my best friend."

"You don't need to explain. It's okay." He hugged me tighter.

The building manager and medics arrived at the same time, and I'm sure we were quite a scene for them: me, hugging a dead body on the floor, a boy hugging me while I hugged the dead body. But I guessed they had seen it all before.

They gently backed me away, and asked me to make a cup of tea. And I went, no questions asked, just like I had been going to make it for Ethel to make her feel better. Timothy followed me into the kitchen. He tried to hug me when we got there, but I pushed him away from me. I filled the teakettle and put it on the stove to heat. I took down a mug, plopped a teabag into it, and set it on the counter. I was on autopilot. Timothy just stood and watched, knowing to keep his distance.

When the kettle chirped, I turned off the stove and poured the steaming water over the bag. I dunked the bag a few times, helping the water flow through. When the tea brewed dark enough, I took it into Ethel's bedroom and tried to hand it to the medic. He looked up at me with a puzzled look on his face.

"It was for you," he said quietly and pushed the mug toward me.

I, with a blank face, stared at him, dumbfounded, and still in shock. Timothy put his hand on my shoulder and steered me out of the room and into the living room, as they strapped Ethel onto a stretcher and pulled a sheet over her body and face.

I collapsed in one of Ethel's reclining chairs and tears continued to pour from my eyes. As the stretcher wheeled passed me, I asked, "What happened?" hoping to get an answer from someone.

A woman medic said, "We won't know until the autopsy.

Could have been a heart attack." Then she asked me if I needed anything or wanted to see a doctor. I said no.

The only thing I needed was Ethel, alive again and laughing.

The doorman and building manager were in the living room now. They told me they were sorry. I wanted to say, "Why? Did you kill her?" But I knew they didn't and that the response would be inappropriate. I just said, "Thanks."

I felt empty but like a couple ton of bricks was pressing in on my chest. My head was spinning and life seemed to move in slow motion.

The doorman walked over to my portrait of Ethel, still sitting on the floor, propped up against the wall, across from her chair, right where I left it. He picked it up and gazed at the canvas. I saw tears form in his eyes.

Then he walked toward me and handed it to me. "She told me it was her favorite picture," he said. "You should have it."

I grasped the picture and stared at it. Ethel, my Ethel. One of the few, maybe the only person, who understood me. And now I had no one. I felt like someone had stuck a draining tube in my heart and sucked out all of the blood. Nothing in my life had ever felt this bad, this wrong.

The building manager and Timothy were having a conversation, but I heard none of it, at least not coherently. My ears, or maybe it was my head, were overcome with a rushing sound and I felt a little faint. I stayed focused on my painting of Ethel, my sweet, caring, loving Ethel.

Eventually, Timothy and the building manager quit talking and then the manager walked to the kitchen phone. Timothy approached me, walked behind the chair, and rested his hands on my shoulders.

"Jess," he said. "Mr. Wilson is calling your mom to come

get us. He thought it would be better than taking the bus."

"Mmmhmm," I said, barely hearing him, or at least his words weren't registering in my brain properly.

"Did you hear me? Your mom is coming to get us." He circled the chair and squatted down so he was my level, facing me. "Jess, look at me."

I raised my line of vision from the portrait and I allowed my eyes to meet his. I sobbed afresh. "Oh, Timothy, she's gone." I hugged the painting to my chest and brought my knees up too. I wanted to curl up into a ball and die.

He kneeled and wrapped his arms around me. "Shhh, it's okay. Let it out."

I soaked his shirt and used many of the Kleenex in a box on the end table near my chair.

When I was all cried out, I pulled back from him and said, "Thanks." And then I kissed him on the lips, lightly. I was ready to go now. I couldn't bring her back by sitting there. I needed to get to my paints.

Luckily, Mom appeared in the doorway then. "Oh, Jess, honey, I'm so sorry." She rushed towards me and enveloped me in a hug.

"Thanks, Mom." I hugged her back.

"Tim, thanks for having them call me. That was the right thing to do." She gave him a hug too, which I'm sure he enjoyed—probably too much. Especially since she was once again Lycra-clad.

The building manager was standing straight and still near the front door. Mom turned to him, flashed her biggest smile, and said, "Thank you so much for taking care of Jess." She grasped his hand in hers.

Then she turned to me and said, "Come on, kid. Let's get you home and cleaned up. Your nose and eyes are all red."

No shit. That's what happens when you cry, I thought. I

said nothing and shook my head. Timothy draped his arm around my shoulder as we walked out of Ethel's apartment. I didn't even try to stop him. We followed Mom partway down the hallway and then I remembered something.

"Be right back," I said and turned back toward the apartment. The building manager was locking up.

"Here," I said, handing him Ethel's golden key, "I won't need this anymore."

He glanced down at it and then looked into my eyes. "Keep it if you want," he said. "As a memento." Then he wrapped my fist around it.

"Thanks," I said and trotted off down the hall where Mom and Timothy were waiting.

The ride home was uncomfortable. I sat with the painting in front with Mom and Timothy sat in the back. Mom doesn't deal well with death, and I knew that, so I excused her blasting of the radio and singing along with it. But, I should have sat in the back with Timothy, at least then his arm would be around me or he'd have held my hand. I needed human touch and comfort right now. I craved affection and warmth: two things I definitely wasn't getting much of from Mom.

When we pulled into the driveway, Mom finally turned down the radio, but left the motor idling, and said, "Are you going to be okay?" She pushed my hair out of my eyes.

"I hope so," I said.

"Well, good," she said and turned around to face Timothy. "Will you take care of our girl?"

"Yes, Mrs. Vander...I mean, Karen."

"Good." She smiled and added, "Okay, well then, I'm off to the gym, which is where I was headed before I had to come get you."

Sorry to inconvenience you, I thought, bitterly.

Timothy and I climbed out of the car and went into the

house. Jim was working late again so we had it to ourselves. I led Timothy straight down the hall to my room. I wanted familiarity and comfort. I needed to be in my own space. I set the painting of Ethel down against my desk, and I flopped on the bed. Timothy sat down gingerly next to me.

"Can I get you anything?" he asked and picked up my hand.

"No. Just lay down with me." I patted the space next to me with my free hand. "Hold me."

He did as I bade and pretty much encased my body with his, as much as he could. It felt good, probably like a womb feels to a fetus—comforting and secure.

I was exhausted. Sad, but too tired to cry. Angry, but didn't know who to direct my anger at. Part of me wanted to die, but the other part of me knew that wasn't what Ethel would want. She'd want me to keep on living and keep on painting. To be true to myself and to my art. To our art. She never got fame or fortune; I was determined to get it for both of us.

I sighed, and snuggled closer to Timothy and fell asleep.

A couple of hours later, I awoke in the same position in which I had fallen asleep. Timothy was still holding me, and his eyes were open. "Are you feeling better?" he asked.

"A little," I said.

"It'll take time," he said and kissed my forehead. And I knew he was right. I just never remembered it hurting this badly before. Not when my stepfather had died; that was mostly numbness. "Now, aren't you hungry?"

Oh yeah. We had missed dinner. And that reminded me. Ethel must have been dead for quite a while; she hadn't even started dinner for us. That brought fresh tears to my eyes, but they didn't fall.

Timothy was right: I was hungry. I got up from the bed. "Yeah, let's get something to eat," I said and wandered toward the kitchen. The freezer yielded frozen pizza, Hot Pockets, and Healthy Choice Entrees, none of which were appealing. But we had to eat something.

"So, what do you prefer?" I held the freezer door open for him.

"Uhhh," he peered in the door and seemed as enthused about it as I felt.

"Or, we have mac and cheese or spaghetti," I said. I opened the refrigerator and found bags of pre-washed spring salad. "With salad," I added.

"Sure, whatever. Mac and cheese sounds good."

I opened the cupboard door and took out the box. Mac and cheese, good comforting staple food. Mom always made it for me when I was younger and sick and home from school.

I turned on the taps and let water fill a 2-quart pan. And then I set it on the stove to boil. Timothy was standing helplessly in the kitchen. He looked like he needed something to do, so I handed him two bowls and said, "Fill these with salad. There may be tomatoes or cucumbers or something in the crisper too."

I reached into the cabinets high above the kitchen sink and pulled down two bottles: vodka and rum. The rum was a better bet, I thought. I grabbed two glasses and poured some of the amber liquid into each.

"Here," I said, handing Timothy a glass. He held the drink up to the light and gazed at it for a moment, looking puzzled.

"Rum," I said. "Drink it." I clinked my glass against his. "To Ethel. Now she can make art eternally." I don't know why I said that. I don't even know if I believed it. The toast was just what popped into my head.

I chugged the rum in my glass and poured myself some more. Timothy was taking the sipping route; I wanted to get drunk. I longed to feel numb.

I dumped the macaroni into the boiling water and handed Timothy the powdered cheese packet. "Here, add milk and butter," I said. I downed my second drink, and made a rather large third one.

"Don't you want to wait until the pasta's done?" he asked.

"I don't give a damn," I replied and burst into tears again. I raced toward the bathroom and locked myself in. I sat on top of the closed toilet lid.

I heard Timothy's footsteps bounding down the hall after me. "Jess? Jess. Please open up. Let me be with you."

"Go away," I said through muffled sobs.

"Come on, Jess. You shouldn't be by yourself right now."

"I'll be right out. Go away and finish dinner." I heard his footsteps retreat. I looked in the mirror at my reflection. My eyes were red and slightly puffy. My nose was red and runny. I was a mess. I splashed cold water on my face and blew my nose. I added mascara to my eyelashes, thinking that that might keep me from crying, if I knew I would turn into a raccoon. I took a deep breath. Pull yourself together, I told my reflection. You can get through this. You have to remain strong. No one can take care of you but you.

With that pep talk, I opened the door.

16

The week after Ethel's death was somewhat of a blur. I was running on pure adrenaline. I got very little sleep because every time I closed my eyes, I saw her dead body.

I painted a lot and visited the museum little. I painted an oil of Ethel in her lavender outfit. I painted an acrylic of Ethel's favorite chair. I made charcoal drawings and pastel pictures and watercolors of things that reminded me of Ethel: Victoria's Secrets pantyhose on some imaginary person's legs, the marquee for Nordstrom's Café, a portrait of Cary Grant in *Arsenic and Old Lace*. I produced art by the shitload, though none of them were masterpieces.

I drank a lot of coffee and a lot of booze. I don't think my mom or Jim even noticed the bottles of rum and Bailey's that were missing from their kitchen liquor supply.

Millie from the museum called around the middle of that week to let me know that the autopsy results were in. Ethel had died from a blood clot. It had apparently let loose and hit her brain. What a way to go, I thought. And then her bruised and battered face and body sprung to mind. I wondered if that was what caused it, what had caused the clot in the first place.

I was pretty certain a beating could trigger something like that. I searched the web when I got off the phone to find out. But I couldn't find anything substantive out.

Millie had also given me the times of the viewings and funeral service. I was sure her son was putting on a huge hoopla, that all of his business associates would be there. But I didn't want to go. If he didn't pay much attention to her in life, I didn't want to see him pay attention to her in death. The museum staff was having a private memorial service for her after hours in Ethel's favorite room in the museum. I would go to that and properly pay my respects.

When I wasn't painting or drinking, I was holed up in my room with my razor. Occasionally I'd slice my wrist to try and relieve some of the pain. It felt good when I did it. The only problem was the relief didn't last. And then I had to do it all over again.

Mom and Jim stayed out of my way. Once I heard him remark, "Well, is she planning on spending the rest of her goddamn life in there? Just being miserable?"

Mom replied, "Shhh. She's hurting, Jim. Hasn't anyone you know ever died?"

"Yeah, but I didn't go moping around for days."

"Well girls are different. She'll come out when she's ready." And that was the end of their conversation. But hearing Mom stick up for me felt good, and I also think it was a first.

One good thing about the dark hole I was in, Jim wanted nothing to do with my despair. He didn't once even try to sneak in my room at night.

Timothy seemed the most concerned about me than anyone. Every day he appeared at my bedroom window, asking
if I'd let him in. Of course, he'd wait until Mom and Jim were
both gone first. And that was fine by me. I'd let him into the
house and into my room. I always offered him whatever I was
drinking and he always refused. He said he was worried I was
turning into an alcoholic. I told him it was just damage control, that my pain was lessened with each drink and that was
what I needed for the moment.

He was so tender and caring. He kept wanting to hold me
and hug me and reassure me that everything was going to be
okay. That I'd get over it, or that we would—together. But
that wasn't what I wanted, at least not always. Kindness has its
place, but occasionally I just wanted to be fucked, good and
hard. And I told him so. I don't know whether he was happy
or hurt. I mean, he was a teenage boy, so a girl saying, "Give
it to me" and meaning it, was a dream come true; but on the
other hand, he knew I was hurting and only asking for it out
of my hurt, out of despair. He wasn't stupid and he knew I
was using him. Thankfully for me, he complied anyway, and
screwed me as hard as I wanted him to—repeatedly.

Once, when we were going at it and naked, he grabbed
hold of my wrist. I squealed. I knew he didn't mean to hurt
me, that he didn't know about the cutting, but it hurt
nonetheless. He stopped his thrusting and turned my wrist,
palm side up in his hand.

"What the hell?"

I pulled my scabbed wrist away.

"Jessica, what happened?"

"Nothing," I said and wouldn't look him in the eyes.

"Did you do that?"

Then it hit me, we had discussed cutting in health class

in eighth grade, along with the unit on eating disorders.

"Umm." I kissed him, trying to coax him away from my wrist and back to what we were doing.

"Not so fast," he said and pulled out of me. "This is serious." He was still lying on top of me, now with his full weight so I had nowhere to go. I had to talk to him.

"It's no big deal," I said. "Come on, I wanna fuck."

"Jessica, it is a big deal. This is dangerous. It could get infected." He picked up my wrist and kissed the cut area softly. "I want you to promise me you will never do this again." He stared at me intently.

"I promise," I said aloud. Silently I added, never to let you see it again. I knew I couldn't stop cutting. Not now, not while I felt so much pain. He just didn't understand.

Needless to say, his discovery curtailed our romantic interlude for that day.

Seven days after Ethel had died, a parcel delivery guy came to the front door. I was the only one home, once again, so I had to answer it. He carried half a dozen large, flat, newsprint-wrapped packages to my front porch and then rang the bell. They were all addressed to me. When I tore the paper on the first one, I realized what they all were: Ethel's artwork. And there was a note attached in an envelope, taped to the back of one of the paintings. In Ethel's loopy scrawl it read:

Dearest Jessica,
If you are receiving this note and my paintings that means I have passed on to the great museum in the sky. Don't weep for me, dear, for I have had a full, love-filled life. I feel

privileged to have met you. You are a talented artist and
quite a fine young woman. Plus, you have a heart of gold,
for befriending an old woman like me, and for keeping her
secrets. Keep painting, I am sure it will reward you with
great success.
Love,
Ethel

I started to cry. God, how I missed her. I carefully carried all of her precious paintings into my room. For once I didn't feel like drinking and I didn't feel like cutting. Warm feelings started to grow inside of me where that hollow, empty place had been. Ethel believed in me. She thought I was talented. She thought I would succeed. I smiled for the first time in seven days.

The following Sunday night, after museum hours, was the memorial service for Ethel. Someone had brought a cake, the same one we had had at her welcome back party. I had brought my oil painting of Ethel in her lavender outfit. I felt its inclusion was one way to usher her presence into the room. Everyone remarked on its likeness to her, how it was identical to her, down to her slightly crooked smile.

All the museum employees and volunteers attended the memorial and each one took a few moments to talk about Ethel. A memory, a fondness, or a thought was shared. One member of the staff read from a book of poetry by Elizabeth Barrett Browning, another read from Robert Frost: both were Ethel's favorite poems. The museum's curator played a piece of music I didn't know the name of on his harp. (That was the first time in person I had ever seen a harp. I didn't realize how big they really were, and how beautiful.) The harp music brought tears to many people's eyes, even more so than people's comments and remembrances. The old security guard talked about the wonderful fund Ethel had established so that inner city kids could participate in an art program. That was news to me. But then again, in many ways, Ethel was a humble and discreet woman, and she had no reason to confide about her financial arrangements to me.

When it was my turn to speak, I wasn't sure what to say. I was feeling quite emotionally unstable and I was shaking. I closed my eyes and took a deep breath and envisioned Ethel's letter to me: her first and her last. I took strength from her words of encouragement.

I opened my eyes, looked around the room from person to person. Most were smiling at me encouragingly, prompting me to say something. I took another deep breath and said, "Ethel was so much to me. She was the grandmother I never had. She was my guardian angel. She always said nice things to everyone and about everyone and only wanted the best for us, for all who knew her." I paused. My brain was reeling. To myself I said, "And all she got was shit in the end. Raped by some thug, beaten to within an inch of her life, and that caused the blood clot that killed her."

Millie, who was standing next to me, wrapped her bony arm around me. "It's okay, honey," she said.

Aloud, I said the only acceptable thing I could think of, and I meant it with every fiber of my being. "And I miss her." Then I burst into tears.

Millie pulled out a lace hanky and handed it to me. "There, there, Jessica. It's okay." She patted me and hugged me closer.

Part of me hated myself. I was turning into a blubbering fool. And in public, no less. The other part of me relished the comfort from the old people around me. They emanated warmth and something else...almost a sense of family, such as I had never known.

After the tributes, we had cake and ice cream, and then the memorial was officially over. Most of the people wanted to get home before it was dark, as they didn't like to drive then. As Millie said, while adjusting her glasses on her face, "Honey, it's hell getting old." And she chuckled.

With the memorial service over, I must admit, I was finding it slightly easier to get on with each day. I hadn't touched a drop of drink since Ethel's paintings had arrived, and I had only cut myself once, and that was on a rough day when my mom and Jim were fighting and I thought I heard him hit her. Of course, I didn't come out of my room to check, because I think I didn't really want to know. Let them deal with their own issues, I thought. They never helped me deal with mine.

Timothy was being sweet and supportive again. He said the art I now was producing looked lighter and happier than it had in a couple of weeks, or maybe longer. I had been creating paintings based on the sunrises and waterfalls and beach scene photos I had taken in Maui. Plus, we were no longer having sex that bordered on violence.

About a week after the memorial service, or maybe it was two, Mom must have noticed the change in me too. (I was somewhat surprised as I honestly felt she paid no attention to me ever, or at least hadn't in a while.)

We were in the kitchen one morning. Jim was out of town somewhere. "I see you're feeling better," she said.

"Yes," I said, adding sugar to my cup of coffee.

"Good. We're going back to Maui next week, you know."

No, I didn't know. "No one told me," I replied, stirring.

"Well, how could we? I mean, you've been locked in your room for weeks." She peered at me over the top of her big fruit smoothie tumbler.

Ah, could be because I was in mourning, I thought. Shit, no one could catch a break around here. "So, are you and Jim just going?" I crossed my fingers under the table.

"No, we are going as a family." She stressed the word "we."

"Oh. When?" I sat at the table, trying to think of a way out of this.

"We leave on Tuesday morning. The tickets are already bought." She put her tumbler down. The thick, pink mixture oozed down the side of the glass.

"Oh."

"So, let's go to the spa again before we go. You could use a spa visit. Your eyes are still puffy from all that crying." That I didn't believe. But I didn't have the energy or the will to argue.

"When?"

"I'll call Raquel and see if she can squeeze us in, this afternoon or tomorrow. Does that work for you?"

"Sure." I had no plans. Summer consisted of only three more weeks. Daily museum visits brought back too many bad memories right now. I had nothing to do but paint, but I wouldn't tell her that. My plans for Jim's condos had been completed immediately upon our return. The only thing left to do there was implement them.

"And maybe we could shop for you for back-to-school clothes." She sucked down the rest of the smoothie.

That was definitely more time with her than I wanted to spend. Besides the last clothes shopping I did, other than buying a dress in Maui, was with Ethel…whom I could shop with no more. Tears sprung into my eyes. Maybe this was Mom's way of trying. She always did deal with everything by shopping…or with sex.

I reconsidered. "Umm, okay. We can shop a little."

"Oh great!" She almost squealed. Not a very grown up sound escaped her lips. She stood and went to the corner cabinet where she kept miscellaneous items. She opened the door and pulled out a stack of cheesy fashion magazines. "I've Post-it noted the things I think we should get you."

Oh no, she had really put too much thought into this. It wouldn't be a shopping trip; it would be a mission to search and secure. And to me that equaled no fun at all.

The three of us returned to Maui when the escrow closed on the two places Jim had bought. We flew into the same airport and rented the same vehicle—at least it looked like the same damn Jeep to me—but this time we stayed at the two-bedroom condo he had purchased. We didn't stay at the villa because he was having some professionals follow my advice and rip up the carpeting throughout and put in hardwood floors in most of the place and colored slate tiles in the bathrooms.

The two-bedroom condo was mediocre at best, or at least the interior was. But we were there to change that. It had an incredible ocean view and wonderful lanais. The décor in the place was tired; everything needed new paint and the furniture had to go and be replaced with newer, hipper, higher quality stuff. I mean, I know we weren't planning on using these places as our vacation homes often, but Jim had big plans for the two places he bought this time.

This particular condo he wanted to turn into a love nest. He had friends and some of them were friends with

Hollywood people. He knew they'd pay big bucks to stay somewhere posh and private, with an emphasis on private, during weekend getaways. That was the clientele he hoped to attract.

He and I had already planned out a color scheme; Mom wanted little part in redecorating. She said she just came along to work on her tan. The old, icky furniture was there when we arrived, some kind of blond bamboo stuff—all of it matching from living room to kitchen to bedrooms to bath. Disgusting! And it was all piled up on the lanais because the flooring contractors, under Jim and the real estate agent's direction, had laid brand new white and black linoleum in checkerboard style all through the house the week before.

Jim had the cleaners come first thing when we arrived. In fact, they met us at the door of the condo. The furniture we ordered in L.A., all of it black leather and chrome, was expected to arrive any minute. In the meantime, Jim arranged for some company like Goodwill to come and cart all the bamboo shit away.

While I supervised the cleaners and re-measured the floors and made new diagrams of where each piece of furniture should go, Mom went to the beach, and Jim went to the building supply store to pick up the gallons of paint and crown molding we had agreed on. We would paint all of the crown molding and window frames the whitest of whites and paint all of the walls, in each room, Chinese red. It would really provide a showplace for the chrome and glass coffee table and dining table and the black leather and chrome dining chairs, couch, and recliners.

A black Jacuzzi tub was already in place in the master suite and a glass-encased shower. This place was gonna rock when we were through. This was so much fun! Maybe I should study interior design in college instead of fine arts or art history. Mom would be happy for me to learn something practical.

Anyway, the cleaners left, the old furniture was removed, and the delivery guy called about the new stuff. Jim still hadn't returned and I could no longer see Mom on the beach. I guessed she went for a walk. I walked through the place aimlessly. My drawings were all done; I knew where everything should go. We needed to go order the new stainless steel fridge and some cooler kitchen hardware, something from Kohler was what I had my eye on. We only had cheap-ass hardware store $20 fixtures. The place was definitely shaping up.

A pounding at the door startled me out of my planning. I looked through the peephole only to see huge pieces of crown molding blocking my view. I opened the door.

"Christ, Jess, could you be any slower?" Jim was NOT in a good mood. I wondered what in the hell happened. I didn't think it took me more than a few seconds from his knock to my opening the door.

I said nothing. He dumped the molding onto the floor in the doorway. I grabbed hold of one end of the bundle and lifted/dragged it out of the doorway.

"You're going to scratch the floors, stupid!" He jerked the wood out of my hand and carried it to the far wall.

"Sorry. I didn't realize how heavy it was," I said defensively.

"Well, pay attention." He turned and stormed towards the door. "There's more shit in the car."

"Do you want me to come with you?"

"No, just stay here and keep the door open. I can get it."

He stormed down the steps and around the building toward the parking lot.

I hated it when he was like this; I felt like I was walking on eggshells. I wished I knew what set him off.

He was back in a couple of minutes with two gallons of paint per hand and stirrers and paintbrushes sticking out of his pants' pockets. He dropped everything on the floor in the doorway once again, but this time I knew better. I picked up the paint cans one by one and carried them into the room.

Jim had said nothing but had thrown the stir sticks and brushes onto the floor and left again, I presumed for more stuff. I was correct as he returned with a saw and a bag of goodies—drop cloths, a container of brush cleaner, painter's tape, etc. I was going to have fun painting this place.

He slammed the door shut and locked it, causing a chill to travel down my spine. That was not a good sign.

He came up behind me and wrapped his arms around me and leaned against me. I could feel his erection against my buttocks. "Jim," I said, almost pleadingly. "Mom could be back any minute."

"Like hell," he grunted. "I just saw her lying on the beach with some cabana boy. He was rubbing oil all over her, feeling her up."

So that's what this was all about.

He cupped my breasts with his hands. "Come on, Jess," he said. "We need to christen this place properly."

"No," I said, trying to sound firm and unafraid, having flashbacks of our other trip to this same island.

"You know you want to." He caressed me, but it was rough, nothing tender about it.

"No," I said again.

"We owe it to this place, to your mom, the two-timing bitch." He was getting angrier now and I was afraid.

"But the furniture delivery guy is coming." I turned to face him, thinking if he could see my eyes maybe he'd understand how I didn't want this.

"Well then he can fucking watch," he said as he pushed me onto the ground, mashed his lips so hard into mine I was sure they were bruised, and raped me.

I didn't fight. I didn't even offer any resistance. I know you are probably thinking that I wanted it to happen, at least by my inactions, but that wasn't the truth. I was just tired of fighting him off. It had never done any good in the past, plus I figured the quicker we got it over with the better: we wouldn't get caught by my mom or by the delivery guys. Plus he'd be in a better mood; the nice Jim would be back. The one who I designed this place with, the one who took care of me and Mom, who when he was nice, he was really nice and caring and loving, not the brute who had attacked me and had forced himself on me and who had forced me to suck his dick.

When he was done, I pushed him off me and raced into the bathroom, determined to get every bit of his semen off me, out of me, away from me. He didn't say anything, just arose and zipped himself back up and went into the kitchen opening up bags, hauling out drop cloths, and spreading them on the now desecrated floor.

By the time I cleaned up and got back to the kitchen, the deliverymen had arrived. The front door was wide open and they were bringing in crated furniture and just setting it anywhere on the covered floor. I hoped Jim remembered to buy a crow bar, otherwise we'd never get the stuff out of the crates.

The guys brought crates up for the better part of a half an hour. I hoped Jim would tip them well. I provided them with icy cans of Coke; it was the least I could do. Then I took over the taping Jim had started as he supervised the rest of the furniture delivery. Mom was still nowhere to be seen.

The rest of the afternoon was fine, though Mom had been gone for hours by then. Jim and I taped, measured and cut crown molding, and painted, agreeing to keep the furniture crated until we were done, so we wouldn't get splashes of paint on it. I was still a little wary, waiting to see if he'd explode again or attack me, but he seemed to be in a good mood. We played some old radio he had found in a closet and sang along to old seventies and eighties songs from Cindy Lauper, Duran Duran, and Steely Dan. We almost had fun, if it wasn't for the hollowness in the pit of my stomach and the slight pain between my legs.

When the sun had sunk, I started to get worried. Certainly Mom should have returned by now. We had the living room, kitchen, both bathrooms, and one bedroom completed—and they looked damn good.

I hesitated to bring up the subject of my missing mother with Jim for fear of setting him off again, so I kept quiet about it and silently pleaded with God, if he or she existed, or with any other supreme being who could hear my thoughts, to send her home safely.

My thoughts were interrupted by Jim, asking if I was hungry. As a matter of fact, I was starving. Diet Coke, water, and a nutrition bar were the only things I had eaten besides some scary airline food—we flew coach this time.

"Good, me too," Jim said, after I said I was famished.

"How 'bout if I call out for pizza and salad? You want anchovies, pepperoni, or what?"

That just goes to prove you can live with someone for a long time and they still might never know you: I was a semi-vegetarian, but I guessed he forgot, or never paid attention.

"Veggies, extra cheese with mushrooms," I said.

"Really? No meat?" He looked perplexed, with furrowed eyebrows and a wrinkled forehead.

"Yes, really. I only eat fish and an occasional piece of chicken," I said.

"Huh. Well, what d' you know? Don't know why I never noticed," he said, turning to the phone and the phonebook on the counter beneath it.

Doesn't surprise me, I thought. You only notice what suits you.

"Well, in that case, I'll order you a large veggie and I'll get a large meat and we'll split a large Caesar salad sans anchovies, okay? What'd you want to drink? A beer?"

"I'm sixteen, Jim. Iced tea is just fine."

"Right," he said with a smile on his face. "And if your mother ever gets back from wherever, she'll just have to fend for herself."

I thought I detected a little malice in his statement so I turned and walked over to the wall, feigning inspection of the new paint job. I didn't want to talk about my mother.

When he got off the phone he said they had promised to be there in 30 minutes. "Why don't we call it a night?" he said. "I'm gonna take a shower and get cleaned up." He grinned.

He better not ask me to join him, I thought and shivered. "I'm gonna start on my bedroom," I said. "I'd love to get it done."

"You work too hard, Jess, but if that's what you want." With that he turned and walked down the hall to the bathroom.

Within a minute he returned, naked except for a towel around his waist, and I tensed until he said, "Here's my wallet," he said, "in case I don't hear the pizza guy."

"Thanks," I said. He walked down the hallway and actually shut the door. I opened the wallet and looked at the wad of twenties and fifties. The leather was stretched, there were so many. I started to count and then figured what the hell, he wouldn't miss a few. I considered it payment for the afternoon—for the work and the other thing I didn't want to think about.

I carried the paint cans into my room, along with an unused drop cloth, and set everything up to go in the morning. I didn't really want to paint anymore. I was tired and my shoulder muscles hurt from using the roller for so many hours. I was used to small muscle and motor painting; this whole room painting was exhausting. I sat on the floor of my room, clasped my knees to my chest, rested my head against them, and tried not to cry.

Mom came traipsing in while we were standing at the kitchen counter eating, as no chairs had been unpacked yet. She was still in her skimpy bathing suit with a sarong around her waist. Her sandals were dangling from her hand. "Hello, all. Ah, pizza." She reached into Jim's box and grabbed a piece.

"Well, well, the prodigal girlfriend and mother has returned," Jim said snidely.

I knew this wasn't going to be good.

Mom glared at him. "What's *your* problem?"

"PROBLEM? I'll give you a problem!" He exploded and slammed his fist on the kitchen counter. "How dare you waltz in here after your daughter and I have damn near worked our asses off all day!"

She grinned at him and carried her slice of pizza down the hallway. "I was busy," she mumbled between bites.

"Busy! Busy? Busy blowin' cabana boys!" Jim stormed after her and slammed the door of their room.

I couldn't figure out if it was better to stay in the kitchen or if I should grab the pizza and make a run for it to my room. Or maybe my lanai would be better—at least outside I might not be able to hear them. Maybe the roaring waves would cover the screaming and fighting I knew was just beginning. If I were at home, I would run to Timothy's to escape the racket.

I opened the pizza box, threw some salad in next to what was left, grabbed my iced tea, and high tailed to my room. After shutting and locking my door, I opened the sliding glass door to the lanai. Then I remembered I had nothing to sit on. I raced from my bedroom to my bathroom and grabbed one of my towels. That would have to do.

I spread that on the terrace and sat cross-legged with the pizza box on top of my lap, stuffing my face with food and trying unsuccessfully to block out what I thought was going on in their room.

After what seemed like a half an hour, I really had to pee. I couldn't wait any longer so I stood, stretching my legs, and crept back into my room, listening. I didn't hear anything through all the locked doors. I opened mine and went out into the hall—the only way to access the toilet.

It was then I heard the noise. It sounded like my mother saying, "Give it to me." I scurried into the bathroom and locked the door. I turned on the shower water, hot, and stripped and climbed in. Another day finished that I didn't want to remember.

After washing whatever I could away from me, I dried my hair, and wrapped myself in a towel to sneak back to my room. Now the noises coming from the master suite were recognizable; I guessed they had made up.

A sleeping bag was spread on the floor since my bed was still in a crate. I lit a couple of candles I brought from home, because I didn't want to turn on the glaring overhead light. I slid my hand into the far corner of my make up bag and my fingers grasped the cool steel of the straight-edged razor I had stolen from Jim.

I played with the razor, turning it flat-edged between my fingers, caressing its smoothness, knowing it had the power to comfort me. I'd be lost without it. I turned over my lily-white right wrist and held it near the candle. I made a small slice to the left of an old scar and large tears rolled down my cheeks. What release!

I thought about Ethel and sliced some more, careful not to cut any of the scars. I had read somewhere that additional cuts into fairly fresh incisions could cause infection. I didn't want a medical mess, just some of the hurt, the anguish to be gone. I wasn't sure how much more I could take.

I took my bleeding wrist and wiped it all over the clean white walls, after all if I wiped it on towels, they would see it. This place would be far from the love nest Jim wanted. It would be a house of pain and I cursed all who would come here. Its sterility and style couldn't erase the anguish that had been created here, that would still be created here.

My eyes were puffy from so much crying. The blood on my arm had started to clot. I knelt on the sleeping bag and put the razor away, in its safe place, for another day. Jim and my mom were silent now. I hoped they'd stay that way. I needed to get some sleep and to cover up my stains, the out-pouring of my sins, first thing in the morning.

I awoke in the sun's first rays and hurriedly started painting, after donning an old t-shirt and shorts. I had one and a
half walls covered before Mom knocked on my door to see if
I was awake. Last night's pain relief was aptly covered so I let
her in. She was wearing dark sunglasses, big ones, and a sexy,
see-through negligee. Not that I wanted to see through it.

"What's with the glasses?" I asked.

"I fell last night." She lowered her head toward the
ground.

"What?" I was incredulous.

"I fell. I was getting out of the bathtub and slipped."

"Take off those glasses." It was a demand. I felt like a parent dealing with a naughty child.

She slowly lowered them. Just off-center of her left eye
was a huge black and blue mark. Actually, it wasn't just black
and blue. It was yellowish and purple and the white of her
eye was now streaked with red veins or arteries or something. It looked like something from a horror movie mask.

"Holy shit," I said before I realized it.

She patted my arm. "It's okay, honey. I slipped. I hit my face on the bathtub spigot as I was going down."

"Ouch," I said, not believing a word of it. "Maybe we should take a picture, just as a reminder not to stand in the tub," I joked. We might need it for the court, when you file your restraining order, I thought.

"Oh, that won't be necessary," Mom sat on my floor. "I won't be doing that again."

"Does it hurt?"

"Only when I try to close my eyes," she said and smiled. "Where's Jim?"

"Still sleeping. He's had a hard night."

Yeah, I'll bet.

"Hey, do you want to go walk on the beach?" I asked, trying to figure out a way to get her out of there, not knowing what kind of mood Jim would be in when he awoke. I was feeling very protective.

"Sure, just let me change. You have any cold pizza left? I didn't get much dinner." She eyed the box with her one good eye.

"Sure. Cold pizza is great for breakfast. You taught me well." I laughed. We had many mornings of cold, leftover pizza after my stepfather died and my mother was going through her depression. I handed her a piece and grabbed one for myself. Half of the pizza was still left.

After she dressed and I changed, we slipped out of the condo and walked quietly along the beach. I loved the ocean; it seemed to have such a healing force with each in and out of the rolling waves.

After walking for a while, bare feet making imprints in the sand, I asked, "Are you happy, Mom?"

"Of course," was her automatic reply.

"No, I mean really happy. Are you?" I had stopped and

was trying to look her in the face, but she wasn't helping me. "Stop and look at me. Are you truly happy?"

She stopped and faced me, dark glasses still covering her eyes. "Why wouldn't I be?"

Maybe because Jim beats on you, I thought. "Well, you and Jim fight a lot."

She chuckled and it sounded forced. "Oh honey, that's just what people do. You're young yet and don't know."

I may be what she considered young, but I did know. People didn't have to act like this. They didn't have to be in relationships like this. We didn't have to live with a man like this. I wanted to scream all these things at her, to make her hear me, to make her understand.

"Maybe not," I said. "But you didn't seem to fight so much with Gene." That was my stepfather's name.

"It's not that we didn't fight. We plain didn't communicate and look where that got me." She crossed her arms across her chest.

"Yes, but he seemed to treat you better." And me too, I silently added.

"What do you mean? Jim gives us everything we need. He buys me all kinds of expensive things. We have a great roof over our heads and now vacation homes. What are you talking about?"

But at what price, I thought. "Mom, stuff isn't everything." I started to walk again because I could see she was getting upset—mad at me to be exact, and that's not what I needed.

"You ungrateful bitch!" She was mad now and I was afraid she'd slap me. "What other teenager gets to go to Maui twice in one summer and gets to decorate condos and offer advice and color schemes and shit?"

"Calm down. I didn't mean that. I just meant that if you

weren't happy, you shouldn't stay with him. I don't mind being poor again."

"Well, I do. Jim is good to me and to you and don't you forget it." She walked faster now, like she was trying to get away from me.

"Mom," I called after her. "I'm sorry." My voice started to crack. "I didn't mean it. I love you and just wanted to make sure you were okay."

She turned and faced me and lowered the glasses. "I told you, I slipped in the tub. Now let's go back to the condo and see if we can't get some furniture crates open so we can start decorating." And she headed back down the beach. Discussion closed.

Jim was awake when we got back and he was frying eggs, something he did very well, surprisingly. "Good morning, ladies," he beamed. I guessed disturbing our peace rocked his world.

"Jess, I saw that you started on your bedroom. Looks good." He smiled. I wanted to smack him, right across his bleached white teeth.

"Thanks," I mumbled.

"What can I do to help?" Mom asked as she wandered into the kitchen and wrapped her arms around him from behind. She still wore the sunglasses.

"Nothing, sweetie. The toast is in the oven since there's no toaster yet. OJ is in the fridge if you want to pour. Jess, I made breakfast for you, too."

"Do I have time for a shower?" I asked, not really wanting to witness this gushy display.

"Only if you do it quickly. The eggs will be ready in one more minute and they're not good cold." He smiled, oozing what he probably thought was charm. I thought it was bull-shit.

"Okay. I'll only be a sec." I really wanted only two things: to put a Band-Aid on my cuts so they wouldn't see them and to throw some cold water on my face. I felt like I was walking around in a nightmare from which I needed to be woken.

When I emerged from the bathroom, the two of them were actually sitting on the floor, feeding food to each other while listening to some cheesy Air Supply songs on the radio. I wanted to puke.

"Jessica, your eggs are getting cold," Mom said when she saw me.

I had no choice but to join them, but I didn't sit too close.

I sat on the floor with my plate on my lap and forced myself to look at the two of them. I felt hatred and something else, something raw. It hit me as I lifted a piece of toast to my mouth. Sorrow. Immense, overwhelming sorrow. I was going to cry again.

I wanted my razor.

"Excuse me for a sec.," I said, as I raced out of the room and back to my bathroom. As I closed the door, I felt it. That stomach lump turned to something sour and started to rise. I just reached the toilet in time. As I retched and retched and retched some more, I heard Mom bang on the door.

"Jess, are you okay?" She sounded really concerned.

"Yeah," I said, weakly.

"You don't seem okay. Can I come in?"

No, I wanted to shout, but knew I couldn't. Instead, I didn't answer and she opened the door.

"What's wrong?" she asked.

Isn't it obvious? I thought. "I'm sick."

"But why?" She held back my hair in its ponytail, so it wouldn't hang in my face.

"I seem to have a stomach flu. Maybe from too much pizza." I smiled weakly at my bad joke. And started to dry heave.

"Maybe Jim should run to the store to get you something for your stomach, some ginger ale and Pepto." She then repeated this, yelling to Jim.

Good, get him out of the house, I thought. "Thanks," I whispered, both to her and to the gods that protect us.

"Or maybe it's the paint fumes," she said. "Maybe you should spend the day out of the house, breathing fresh air. We could all go hiking in one of the rain forests."

The hiking part sounded great; being with them all day didn't.

"Ummm...I don't know if it is the paints. Maybe it's really the pizza. I should probably just lie down. Why don't you and Jim go hiking if you want? I can stay here and relax and maybe do a watercolor or something." My heaves had stopped so I flushed the toilet, stood up, and grabbed the mouthwash. What a gross taste in my mouth! It's hard to imagine that something that tastes so good when you eat it could taste so foul coming back up. Why the hell is that?

"Well, if you don't want to, you don't have to. It was just a thought. I figured we could all use a break."

What the hell did she need a break from? She didn't do any work yesterday. "I appreciate that, but I'd just as well stay here."

"Suit yourself," she said and went off to the kitchen to load the dishwasher or at least that is what it sounded like she was doing.

I stayed in the bathroom and took a long look in the mirror. "Jess," I said to myself, "just what *are* you doing?" I shook my head and once again splashed cold water on my face.

When Jim returned from the store with all kinds of stomach ailment remedies for me, he vetoed my mother's idea of hiking. "Karen, we really have to get this shit done. We need to unpack the furniture and finish Jess's room. I need to go over to the villa and see if the floor guys are doing their jobs. I don't have time for an effing hike."

Mom looked like her feelings were hurt, but she said nothing. She put a smile on her face and asked cheerfully, "Where do you want me to start?"

I laid on the living room floor for a while watching them, too weak to really do anything. Jim used a crow bar to open the crates and then he and Mom lifted the furniture out of the crate and put it onto the floor. Then Mom unwrapped it. I couldn't believe how strong she was. All those hours spent in the gym were really paying off now. She had no problems heaving the heavy couch or any of the other larger pieces. My wimpy string beans that I called arms would have been of little help.

When I finally had enough ginger ale in me to have a sugar high, I got up off the floor and started to help unwrap the furniture. It was in bubble wrap and some kind of plastic wrap that took scissors to carefully slice holes big enough that the casing could be pulled off.

The furniture was beautiful and looked just as it did in the catalogues we ordered it from. We had seen very few of the pieces on the designer's showroom floor. Jim seemed pleased. Mom lauded me on the excellent choice. The positive attention made me content.

Around lunchtime, we had the living room completely

set up, plus their bedroom and the dining room. Only my room was left. Mom suggested we stop and she and I run out and pick up take out Chinese.

Jim said, "Great idea and then tonight, if we get this all done, I'll take you both out somewhere nice to celebrate."

"Oh good," Mom squealed like a little girl.

It's started again, I thought. They fought; he spent money on her. I predicted she would get a piece of jewelry tonight at dinner.

"While you're out, maybe you ladies should buy new dresses for the occasion," Jim suggested, pulled out his wallet, and handed Mom a wad of cash.

Yep. I was correct. It was definitely the start of a new cycle. The same old dance repeated. It was a merry-go-round I wanted off of.

"Thanks, honey. I love you," Mom cooed as she kissed him way too passionately in front of me—with tongue. "What do you say, Jess?" she asked me when she stopped slobbering on him.

"Thanks, Jim." I couldn't look him in the face.

"Now, you be nice and give him a hug," she said, hands on her hips, still wearing those damn sunglasses.

Ugh! I did as I was told but didn't enjoy a minute of it. He patted my ass as I walked away. Mom was already in the doorway with the door open so she didn't see. I turned my head and glared at him and muttered under my breath, "Go to hell." Then I walked out the door.

We went to a little boutique that sold Hawaiian print dresses and silver jewelry. Mom found many dresses that she loved, but then again, she loved shopping in general. She dragged me into the dressing room with her, having the salesperson follow with a pile of clothes for each of us. I didn't pick my pile as much as I was told, "Jess, you simply must try this on" for each and every item in my size Mom picked up.

I figured I'd humor her and go along with it. After all, she was in a store and in her glory. She deserved it after last night, no matter what had happened between her and the cabana boy.

She quickly stripped and when she did I noticed something. Or a lot of somethings to be precise: bruises. She had some on her ass that looked like they were caused by indentations from fingers. She had quite a colorful fist-size bruise fading on her thigh; I don't know why I never noticed it before. She must have seen me staring—how could I not—because she said, "Oh, the bruise."

I wasn't sure which she meant, there were so many in various forms of fading. "I usually cover those with self-tanning cream. Pretty smart, huh?"

And she actually looked proud of herself. "Uh, yeah. Where'd they come from?" As if I didn't know.

"Oh, I've been kind of clumsy lately. Don't know what's gotten into me." She smiled weakly.

Yeah, right. I stared at her, not sure if I really knew her. Where was the woman who loved her body, who flaunted her body? "Mom, some of those look kind of bad." I reached towards her to touch a few of them but she stepped away.

"Yeah well, sometimes Jim and I like it rough." She shrugged her shoulders and grinned sheepishly.

"That looks a little too rough to me."

Now she looked embarrassed and possibly angry. "Oh, you're 16. What do you know?" And she slipped a dress over her head. "Try something on."

Conversation closed then.

I quietly undressed and put on the first garment in my pile. It was rayon or something and black and way too muumuu on me. "Ick."

"Yes, definitely not you. What about this?" She held up the next one in my pile, an ocean-blue, spaghetti strapped number, kind of long and a little iridescent. I wasn't too sure.

The dress she had on was sexy and clingy and royal purple, not a color I saw her wear a lot of, but she looked stunning.

Except when she took off her glasses—the dress matched her eye, which seemed to be turning more purple and yellow now and less black and blue.

"Shit!" she said, staring into the mirror. "Do you think I can apply self-tanner that close to my eye?"

I didn't have the heart to tell her that all the self-tanner in the world wouldn't cover that shiner. "Uh, I don't know. What about this?" I had the blue one on now and I actually looked good, or as good as I could look.

"That's it," she said. "Perfect." She whipped off the purple dress and tried on the rest of the dresses in her pile. But none of them even came close to that sexy one, so shiner or not, the purple one was it. She had her sunglasses back on when we came out of the dressing room so the saleslady wouldn't see her eye.

"Jess, these earrings would be fabulous with your dress." She held up a sterling pair with tiny royal blue beads. They looked like lapis lazuli. "And do you have proper shoes?"

I wasn't quite sure what she meant by proper. Did she mean shoes other than tennis shoes? If so, I had black sandals with me. I said as much.

"Oh, but these blue, strappy sandals with the heels would

be so much better." She held them up for me to see and I had to agree. In the end, we each bought a dress, earrings, and a pair of shoes, with what I had silently dubbed Jim's blood money.

We grabbed steamed rice, General Tso's Chicken for them and garlic veggies for me, plus tea, egg rolls, and fortune cookies and headed back to the condo, where I was certain Jim was hungry and impatiently waiting.

19

Dinner went smoothly with no one getting drunk or fighting or causing a scene. I wanted to cause one but I acted properly and refrained. Jim was very attentive to both of us and kept referring to us as "his two girls", which really gave me the willies. And I was correct about the jewelry for Mom. Between the dinner and dessert courses, he pulled a velvet box out of his jacket pocket and placed it in front of her. She opened it to reveal a gorgeous, fiery opal ring. The stone must have been close to ten carats, if not more. It had beautiful pinks, greens, and blues in it. There were also two diamonds, probably a half-carat each on both sides. Must have set him back a bundle. I briefly wondered if us being sent out to buy new dresses was just a ploy to give him time to run to the nearest jewelers.

Then he surprised me, and I think Mom, too, by placing another velvet box in front of me. This one was smaller, but only slightly. My hand was shaking as I opened the box. I didn't want anything from him; I knew its price.

"Come on, Jess. Open it. Show me what it is," Mom said.

I gasped when the lid had sprung. Inside lay two of the most perfect diamond studs I have ever seen. "A carat total," Jim said. "Do you like them?"

How could I not? "They're beautiful!" I exclaimed. I couldn't help myself.

"Just like you, my soon-to-be stepdaughter."

That brought me to a reeling halt. What the hell did he just say? I looked up at them, sitting across from me. Mom and Jim were holding hands. "That's why we wanted to go to dinner tonight, Jess. To celebrate. Jim asked me to marry him and I said yes."

I grasped my water glass and took a drink, not knowing what to say. But I choked on the water and it came out my mouth and nose. Not very elegant. I was embarrassed.

"Well, congratulations," I said, thinking of a multitude of reasons why them getting married wasn't a good idea. In fact it was the worst idea I had ever heard.

"Thank you. We knew you'd be happy." Mom squeezed Jim's hand and was beaming. I was glad she was happy, but I thought she was deluding herself. And I certainly didn't want that bastard for a stepfather. Something would have to be done. I just didn't know what.

Jim ordered a bottle of Cristal with dessert and chocolate Bailey's soufflés, the house specialty, all around.

While we ate dessert Jim announced, "I bought you those earrings because I want you to know that I'm not just marrying your mom. I'm marrying you, too, in a way, because I want us to be a family."

I almost gagged on my soufflé. Disgusting pig. Fucker. Who did he think he was!

"Isn't that sweet, Jess?" Mom's eyes pleaded with me.

Yeah, about as sweet as a lemon. I so wanted to scream and throw my crystal fluted glass in his face, in her face too if she actually thought this was a good idea. Didn't she know what he was doing to me? Didn't she care? And what about her—what he was doing to her? Didn't it matter? What the hell was wrong with her?

I mustered my strength and said, "Excuse me, that stomach thing I had this morning seems to be back." I raced as quickly as I could to the restrooms, leaving the earrings just sitting on the table for them to pick up. I wasn't planning on rejoining them in the restaurant dining room. And if I could have figured out a way to never join them again, I would have.

I was in the bathroom, squatting on the floor of a stall, with my head over the toilet when I heard my mom say my name. My legs were killing me but there was no way I was sitting or kneeling on a public restroom floor, even if it was in a posh restaurant.

"Yes?" I said softly.

"Are you okay?"

"Ummhmm."

"Can I come in?"

"No. I'm coming out. I'm done here. Nothing left in me." Nothing but fury, I thought. I had to do something to get rid of that awful sour taste. "Do you have gum?" I stood slowly, afraid I'd be woozy.

"Yes. I have your earrings, too. Aren't they beautiful? Isn't Jim the best?"

The best *what*? Son of a bitch came to mind. I murmured, "Ummhmm" just to shut her up.

I opened the stall door and looked her over. Her face

appeared old, older than I had ever seen her look. She had tried to cover the shiner with makeup or self-tanning lotion or something. It was sort of covered, but you could definitely see all the orange-colored makeup—very unnatural. I guessed I hadn't noticed in the dim restaurant lights. The ones in the bathroom were bright.

"Here's your gum." She came toward me.

I was thankful and shoved it in my mouth.

"Do you need to see a doctor? That flu you have seems bad." She looked concerned and actually brushed back my hair from my face with her hand.

"No. It'll pass. I'm sure." I hoped it would. I needed to figure out a way for the circumstances to change. I knew that was the only thing that would help my stomach, not to mention the rest of me, and her too.

"Jim's waiting in the car," she said and turned and looked at the bathroom door.

Let him wait, I thought. "Okay," I said. "Just let me splash some cool water on my face. I feel like crap."

She waited in silence while I did that, and then she handed me a paper towel. After drying myself, I followed her out the door and wondered how she couldn't hear my heart: it pounded rapidly. I took a deep breath and tried to calm down and wondered if a heart could pound so hard it could explode.

She said nothing as we walked to the car.

Jim asked if I was feeling better, but that was all during the whole ride back to the condo. I had nothing to say to them.

They went straight to their bedroom; I went to the kitchen. I searched the closet for Saltines, thinking they might help me. I noticed a large wooden knife block, left by the past tenants, on the kitchen counter. The largest knife called to me; I swear I heard it speak my name.

I gave up my cracker search, grasped the knife's wooden handle, and walked quickly to my room and locked the door.

I felt inspired. My memory flashed to a time when I was in preschool and we did art projects. We colored a whole page in crayon, all different colors. Then we colored over the bright colors with black crayon. Next we scraped through the black crayon, creating an outline of a picture. The underneath colors showed through making an incredible scene—darkness with bits of light, bits of color shining through.

Yes. That is what I had to do.

I reached into the closet and pulled out an acrylic I had done the week before. For some unknown reason, I had packed the painting into my suitcase and brought it with me. It was all pinks and reds, just swirled into an abstract. I propped it against my collapsible easel. I pulled out an old brush and some black acrylic paint and covered the canvas entirely. I hoped it would dry quickly.

While I sat and waited, I played with the kitchen knife. I tested the sharpness of the blade with my index finger. I liked the coolness of the steel and its smoothness. It reminded me of a larger version of my razorblade. Except this size knife could do a lot more damage. That made me smile. Damage—now there was a thought. Maybe damage was what I needed. Or more like damage control. Could this knife help me control the damage being inflicted upon us, upon my mother and me?

I got angrier just thinking about it.

The black paint was dry. I took the big knife over the canvas and without slicing the cloth, I scraped a heart into the black. The fuchsias and reds shone through, making a somewhat iridescent outline of a heart. I cut jagged lines through the middle of the heart, to make it break. I attempted to pour my anger, my hurt, my frustrations into the canvas. I scratched an arrow piercing the heart and then another one and another one and another. The heart should bleed. I put the knife to the canvas to scratch drops of blood, but I realized that wasn't what it needed. It needed real blood, genuine droplets. I turned the paint-covered knife to my own wrist and slit—but not too deeply. I squeezed the cut to make drops drip onto the canvas, right where I wanted them, right under the arrows. The blood looked three-dimensional and somewhat ghastly on the canvas. It definitely evoked an emotion. I thought of my art teacher and how proud he'd be of me, always telling me to make sure the viewers feel something when they see the painting. Well, viewers of my work, my masterpieces, would always feel something. I made sure of that.

I wrapped an old t-shirt around my bloody wrist to try and curb the flow. I started to get light-headed and realized losing blood was probably not a good idea on top of spewing all the dinner. But, what the hell, the slicing of my skin actually brought a moment of relief, as did creating another masterpiece.

But then when I realized that, I also realized that I shouldn't need this kind of release. I shouldn't be living this kind of life. And I got angry again. Furious, in fact. Hot tears rolled down my cheeks. I punched the sleeping bag and my pillow.

Shit, shit, shit, I said to myself.

What could I do? I couldn't let Mom marry the bastard. And she didn't look like she wanted him to go away. But I certainly couldn't live with him. And she shouldn't either.

I twirled the knife handle around and around in my hands. The parts of the blade without paint and blood reflected the overhead light. At one point I even saw a distorted version of my face, puffy from crying, and all tense and troubled. My eyes looked very dark.

I had to do something. We couldn't live like this. I couldn't live like this, and I shouldn't. I closed my eyes as tight as I could and saw white spots, almost flashes.

The pain in my chest and behind my eyes was unbearable. I didn't think I could breathe. And that sour taste was back in my mouth.

I *had* to do something.

I could kill myself. That might even offer me instant fame. Many great artists were unknown until they died. Maybe that would afford me my fifteen minutes of fame.

But then again, Mom wouldn't know what the hell to do with my stuff, and Jim would probably just burn it or send it to the dump. Including all of my and Ethel's artwork.

And as much as Mom and I didn't have a close relationship, I knew how she had reacted to Gene's death; I just couldn't do that to her again.

And that was just it. She needed me to protect her and if I wasn't here, I couldn't protect her. She'd be left to fight the bastard all by herself. And in her mourning, she wouldn't have the strength. Hell, she didn't even have the strength now. She needed me, even if she'd never admit to it.

Well, then, that settled it. That left me with only one choice. And I hoped she'd see it that way and understand. I would do it for the both of us, but mainly for her. She deserved better. She deserved to be safe. If she couldn't provide safety for us, I could. And I would.

He deserved torment and hell after all the shit he'd put us through.

I clenched the knife, got up off the floor, opened my door, and turned off my light.

Jill L. Ferguson spent the second half of the 1990s being a personal safety, domestic violence and substance abuse educator and consultant, working with many schools, government agencies and nonprofit organizations.

She currently chairs the General Education Department at the San Francisco Conservatory of Music, where she teaches creative writing, literature and communication. Over 600 of her articles, essays and poems have been published in magazines, newspapers and books. This is her first novel.